To Die This Day

The rich and powerful Traffords are both proud and relieved when their eldest son, Tom, returns home safely to the family ranch after the war. When his wartime partner and hero, Clayton Grady, shows up too, the homecoming celebrations rock the county.

How could veteran Grady know that this seemingly happy event would in time tear his family apart and lead to a nightmare of deceit, suspicion and bloody murder, as horrific as anything he had encountered during the war. . . .

To Die This Day

Clint Ryker

A Black Horse Western

ROBERT HALE · LONDON

© Clint Ryker 2010
First published in Great Britain 2010

ISBN 978-0-7090-8861-5

Robert Hale Limited
Clerkenwell House
Clerkenwell Green
London EC1R 0HT

www.halebooks.com

Typeset by
Derek Doyle & Associates, Shaw Heath
Printed and bound in Great Britain by
CPI Antony Rowe, Chippenham and Eastbourne

ONE

HUNTED MAN

It seemed to young Lee Clarke that whenever somebody was feeling poorly on the Maverick these days they took it out on him.

The job he'd just completed on the windmill was a prime example. Big Tom had ordered him to get on with the chore of patching up the sluice trough directly after the noon break, which he'd done. It had taken all afternoon and even if it wasn't as good a job as his Uncle Luke or Old Kentucky might have done, it was the best he could do and he reckoned that should have been good enough.

But it wasn't.

Tom hadn't said anything yet, but Lee sensed he

was about to. He could tell by the look on his brother-in-law's face as he circled the trough in the scorching heat with his hands thrust in the back pockets of his pants, chewing a blade of grass, frowning.

That same look had been on the big man's face when he quit the house that morning in a huff after his argument with Virna – and that of course was the cause of his bad mood. Lee's sister and Tom, her husband, had had a tiff, so Tom was about to take it out on him. That was the pattern on Maverick that summer, and Lee reckoned it was no way to run any outfit.

He swabbed sweat from his face and waited.

The steady wind coming in off the desert carried no coolness. It barely kept the windmill spinning, just stirring the dust and blistering everything it touched. In the distance to the west the metal rooftops of the ranch house and mine buildings shimmered like molten silver. Lee envisioned an ice-cold pitcher of lemonade at his side as he stretched out lazily in the deep shade of the veranda.

Eventually Big Tom turned and looked at him directly. Here it comes, the boy thought. The big lecture. But before the man could say anything, they heard the sound from far off to the north-east, a low muttering of noise beneath a brassy sky. Like summer thunder. Or maybe gunfire.

'What's that, Tom?' he asked, welcoming anything that might divert attention from his attempt at hardly professional carpentry. 'Sounds like shooting.'

The boss of the Maverick Ranch and Maverick Mine, a big man by any standards, swung his head and cocked his ear to the barely discernible sounds. He scowled as he indicated the smoky blue smudge on the horizon that was the outline of the Battle Valley Hills.

'Can't you see the clouding forming over them hills?' he said grumpily. 'That's just a summer thunderstorm. Use your eyes, boy, use your eyes.'

Boy!

Sometimes that was hard to take. When Uncle Luke used the term, it somehow had a very different meaning. Tom made it sound like he was just a fool kid who had to be told every little thing.

Lee didn't reply straight away.

Instead he dipped his hands in the trough. The water was warm yet still cooler than that hot wind. He tossed his hat aside, lowered his head and splashed water over his face. This felt so good he scooped up handfuls and let it run through his thick dark hair and down his neck.

'That was clever,' Tom remarked. 'You'll be hotter than ever once you start to dry.'

With his face still dripping, Lee stared at the big man and held down his irritation. He knew he was likely asking for trouble in contesting this, but it was better than discussing the water trough.

'At least I'll be cool for a minute or two,' he said. He shook his head and the water sprayed off him to hit the ground in little drops that dried instantly. Then, as that faint, far-off sound came again, he frowned. 'Doesn't sound like thunder to me, Tom.'

With the air of someone burdened with enough problems without having to put up with half-grown boys who couldn't tell the difference between gunfire and summer thunder, Big Tom Trafford walked to his horse and swung up. That was enough to bring him out in a fresh sweat. He tugged off his hat, and swabbed his brow with a kerchief.

'I've got work at the mine, boy,' he said finally. 'Tidy up here, then get back to headquarters. Your sister has some chores she wants taken care of.'

'Yes, sir!' Lee answered, putting as much sarcasm into his voice as he dared.

The other rode off and Lee sighed and turned back to the trough. Maybe, he mused, one of the big advantages of being adult was that you got to vent your spleen on seventeen-year-olds. He only hoped there was some junior around on the Maverick for him to bully when he was old enough to call the shots.

He was collecting his tools when another rumble of stuttering sound came washing across the far reaches of the desert, causing him to straighten and stand staring intently off to the north-east towards that blue line of heat-stricken hills.

He didn't care what Big Tom said. That still sounded like gunfire to him.

The dust rose in a thick, rolling mass behind him, moving as if possessed by an energy all its own. Closing in on the Sawbuck Hills on the vast desert plain, Clayton Grady rode low on the neck of the black stallion as he touched lathered flanks lightly with spur.

Gunshots thundered from behind but the tall rider didn't bother to duck. His pursuers were still out of range, and he had but to turn his head to see spent bullets slashing the earth well behind.

Grady swung his gaze ahead.

The scene before him was as clear-cut as an etching.

Scrub-dotted plain with cloud-shadowed hills flanked the plain away to his left. Farther on loomed mountains where a man could likely shake off his pursuers and hide. And now that rolling cloud of hoof-lifted dust was moving at an angle that could eventually cut him off from reaching the Battle Valley Hills if hunted and hunter both maintained course and pace. The bastards wanted to catch him out here on the open plain where they could shoot him down like a dog.

The hell they would!

Grady had survived blackwater fever in Louisiana, four years of war, and countless close shaves in the years since Appomattox. A man with that sort of record wasn't about to lie down and die like a dog out here in the nameless Arizonan desert – or so he reassured himself. Yet a further two miles saw his hard-riding pursuers slowly but surely narrowing the gap. The bullets were still kicking up the dust behind him, yet not as far back as before. They were trying to panic him, waiting for him to do something stupid.

His smile was defiant, teeth flashing whitely. This was far from the first time someone had underestimated Clay Grady.

The sun was sloping low and long shadows came reaching far across the open plain.

The horseman wanted to believe he could stay ahead until darkfall, but at last realized he couldn't. He had selected the black stallion for flashy looks, not staying power.

By contrast his pursuers were mounted on runty Texas mustangs which could run all day and then back up for a long night ride on nothing more than a swallow of water and a handful of corn.

The cloud-topped Battle Valley Hills now appeared tantalizingly close, yet still unattainable. Then suddenly the terrain altered dramatically with the landscape ahead abruptly breaking up before him into a series of canyons and twisted arroyos flanked by gaunt stands of mesquite and dogwood.

Grady grimaced and touched gunbutt. He was good with a Colt, maybe brilliant. But the men behind were no rubes either. If it came down to guns – as more and more it was beginning to seem that it must – then he would surely need some advantage to help offset the odds.

Another racing mile saw him focusing upon an arroyo off to the right. It appeared to be invitingly deep. By this his flashy mount was blowing hard and beginning to slow badly. The whole plain now lay in shadow yet full dark was still an hour away.

They could run him down in that time.

So it must be the arroyo.

He jerked hard on the right-hand rein and the stallion swerved and angled across a weed-tufted saltpan. Over his shoulder the rider saw his hunters instantly change direction to follow.

The noise of the black's hoofs piled echoes atop one another as they entered the arroyo. Gaunt and broken walls of tortured rock rose on either side, and Grady felt his heart leap when he realized the bed of the arroyo directly ahead was cluttered with boulders and clumps of saltbrush.

Natural cover!

He raked viciously with spur now. The black grunted in protest but somehow managed to lift its gait just a little as muffled cursing and shouting sounded from behind when they saw he could make cover.

A tense half-mile flowed by with Grady following the winding course of the arroyo at a reckless pace, ducking beneath clawing branches and weaving between the boulders with dust boiling thickly in his wake.

He knew the dust had to be confusing his pursuers, yet somehow they kept coming. He scanned the terrain ahead through narrowed eyes and finally sighted what he was looking for.

A short distance ahead the arroyo curved sharply right and he could see the tops of much larger boulders just around the bend.

Right away he knew he'd found the right place to make his stand.

He let the reins drop upon the animal's sweating neck and plucked the Bowie knife from his belt. Bending low, he slashed the cinch strap as the animal slowed while taking the bend in deep sand. Dropping the knife, he seized the pommel in both hands and allowed the mount's turning motion to throw him clear with his burden.

He hit ground with the heavy saddle held before him to break his fall. The lathered black horse, now freed from his weight, jumped a deadfall branch and raced away.

Grady figured he somersaulted twice on impact – maybe three times. But he'd prepared for it and he knew how to fall. When he eventually came to rest, dazed and dust-coated, he was still clutching the saddle to him as fiercely as a sailor holding his woman after two years at sea.

Such concern for saddlery under the circumstances might have appeared suicidally foolish to an onlooker. But it made the best kind of sense to the man with maybe the most valuable saddle in the county.

The beat of hoofs drummed closer.

With a shake of his head and an iron set to his jaw, Grady made it to his feet and began to run. A dozen long strides carried him toward two large boulders which leaned together like exhausted workmen. He hurled the saddle in back of the boulders then dived after them headlong to land in soft sand. The instant he came up onto one knee his hand smacked the ivory butt of his Colt .45 and jerked the weapon clear.

His face was grim as he faced back the way he had come. Gone was that reckless grin that had marked so many hair-raising passages of his life to be replaced by a mask so murderous it might scare a rabid dog.

The gunhammer clicked back softly, a small sound that was engulfed by the rising drumbeat of hoofs as the three horsemen came storming around the bend into the arroyo.

In a moment of heightened clarity Clayton Grady saw in vivid detail the men who wanted so desperately to kill him. Leathery, hard-bitten men with stubbled jaws, gleaming cartridge belts and naked guns. Outlaw scum.

The lead rider hollered and reined in on spotting the riderless horse which had trotted on a hundred yards farther before halting. Grady's Colt crashed and the bullet smashed the leader's face, killing him before he could make one sound.

He swung the smoking gun after the second rider only to realize the man had slipped down the offside of his horse to hang on with one boot hooked around the saddle pommel, Indian style, while his henchman started in shooting.

Forced low, Grady rolled several yards with bullets ricochetting off rock all about him but none even coming close, so fast did he move.

Suddenly he went belly-flat with the smoking Colt extended to arms' length before him to present a minimal target. By contrast, the surviving two riders made huge targets.

He didn't miss. Couldn't.

Three soft-nosed slugs exploded the third rider's face into a geyser of crimson and it was an all but headless *thing* that tumbled to earth and rolled. Almost too late, Grady realized the grotesque corpse was bouncing directly toward him while the horse slewed wildly aside.

He rolled violently and almost got clear. Almost. The tumbling corpse crashed across his legs and pain jolted up his spine. He locked his mind against it and was kicking his way free when hands wrapped around his throat and through a fog of sand and gunsmoke he realized the second rider had somehow lost his weapon so had dived headlong from his mount to seize him with bare hands from behind.

Hands like vices upon his throat.

He was choking as he struggled to fight back. He would never know how he managed to kick a leg free of that dead weight encumbering him, but knew exactly what he was doing when he pistoned his knee upwards with all his strength.

And felt the violent contact of bone against bone.

His attacker howled but didn't loosen his grip. Grady was all but unconscious by this. His hand scrabbled wildly in the sand. He grabbed a rock and struck out feebly. Yet the pressure on his throat only increased as the darkness surrounding him intensified.

He was choking to death!

Miraculously, his clawing fingers brushed something metallic. The gun he'd dropped! Blindly he seized the familiar curve of the ivory butt. He was choking and half sobbing now but didn't even know it. The only reality was the gun. It weighed a ton as he brought it up, the blackness in his head now shot through with streaking starbursts of vermilion and crimson.

Was he dying?

The hell he was!

Somehow he rammed the gun muzzle hard into the outlaw's belly and jerked trigger. The shot was muffled but the great weight instantly fell away, leaving him coughing feebly, his throat a tube of fire. When his vision slowly began to clear he realized he was sitting up in the sand and blinking about owlishly, that ominous darkness at last beginning to clear from his head.

The man who'd come so close to killing him lay on his back close by, jaws locked in the final rictus of death. The first one he'd shot was sprawled lifeless where he'd fallen, legs and arms akimbo, face mercifully hidden.

'Burn in Hell!' he spat, and sleeved lips with a shaking arm before mustering the strength to rise.

It was agony to come erect, an act of iron will to get numbed legs moving.

The saddle was an impossible weight, but he wouldn't leave it. Could not. He got it off the ground with his third desperate attempt, lurched sideways against a bullet-scored boulder, fell to his knees but somehow clawed his way upright again.

How dark it seemed now!

Everything appeared shadowy, ill-defined. That warmth flooding his chest was blood, he knew. His blood. Settling dust continued to come down over him as he moved off – away from the dead and the man who might still be alive, who might even at that very moment be lining him up in his gunsights for all he knew.

Each time he rose he fell again, yet each succeeding step raised his hopes. The belly shot man must be dead, he assured himself. He knew his lead had gone deep. But Conrad was a tough one. Tough, and mean as dirt. He would come after him and kill him if there was one breath left in his body. So Grady would keep going. He must.

Soon he found himself climbing. The arroyo wall was covered with loose shale and his boots kept giving way. His mouth was parched and his throat swollen, the pain in his lungs brutal now. He hated the saddle by this but wouldn't leave go. When forced to clamber upwards on hands and knees, he dragged it behind him. The arroyo was now silent in the aftermath of the violence. Gasping for breath, he paused and looked around. He saw a dark crack in the rock-face of the arroyo, almost hidden behind a mesquite tree. He tore the saddle lining open and with bruised, shaking hands he pushed the bank notes deep into the crevice, covering the narrow opening with a fallen branch. He turned and clambered up the cliff face.

Abruptly there was level ground beneath him and Grady gratefully rolled over onto his back on the sand and lay motionless staring straight up into a darkening sky.

The stars were out by the time he eventually stirred again.

The bullet wound was serious enough, yet he knew he'd survived much worse. He strapped his chest tightly with strips from a torn-up shirt and fortified himself from the whiskey flask he took from his saddle-bags. The nameless arroyo was now a dark gash across the desert floor and nothing stirred within its gloomy depths.

For the first time in a desperate hour the reckless smile returned as he slung the saddle over his shoulder and began to walk.

His famous luck had held again!

It was after midnight before he stumbled upon the stone section marker and proceeded to read it by the light of a bright Arizona moon. He sat down smiling upon his saddle and told himself this had to be his double-lucky day.

For the sign read: MAVERICK RANCH – his destination!

TWO

NEW MAN ON MAVERICK

Luke Trafford stood on the ranch house porch watching the sun come up out of New Mexico.

He was a tall young man with wide shoulders and an easy manner which made him the most popular man on Maverick Ranch. To the cowboys who worked the spread, and the diggers in the Maverick Mine, he was such an easy man to like that at times they tended to forget he was the boss-man's brother.

Big Tom Trafford was certainly respected on Maverick, but scarcely well-liked. Yet the hands were never critical of the older brother when Luke was around for he was a man who held family high, was ever ready to stand up for relatives whether they be right or wrong.

The sun was gathering strength as it cleared the mesa rim to spill its hot light over the sprawling Trafford kingdom of grass and cattle.

Luke watched as the distant Capitan Mountains changed colour from purple, to blue and finally a misty grey. Then there came a stirring from within the bunkhouse and a thin tendril of smoke began rising from the cookhouse chimney where Tad Gruber was rattling his pots and pans.

The ranch headquarters sprawled across a buffalo-grass rise with a heavy stand of cottonwoods in back. A slender stream separated the out-buildings from the mine. Men had ranched here on the fringe of Lizard Desert for years but the Maverick Mine had only been in operation since the day two years back when Tom had driven a pick into the earth at the base of Squaw Mesa and sighted something glinting golden embedded in the hard grey stone.

Ever since that day, ranching on the Maverick had taken second place to mining, although Tom Trafford still regarded himself as a cattleman first and a miner second.

Luke often reflected on his brother's attitude in

this regard. He sensed that because Tom regarded ranching as a right and proper way to make a living for any Arizonan, he chose to regard himself this way.

Nonetheless, Tom Trafford took the mining operation very seriously. All on the spread knew it could never have become so successful on cattle alone, that the fact that the outfit now had twice the number of men working underground as on the spread itself was proof that the senior brother knew exactly where their priorities lay.

A tall and grizzled figure emerged from the number one bunkhouse to stand stretching and scratching for several minutes before starting across the yard for the house.

Old Kentucky was the only hand on Maverick who ever got to dine with the family.

Nobody knew how old he really was, nor where he'd come from that day he came riding in on a worn-out claybank during the Traffords' early days on the spread to slot in immediately with the family like he'd been part of it all his life.

He was a lean and hardy man who could work side by side with the youngest and fittest on the place all day long, then sit up and spin yards about his 'feudin' days' back in Kentucky for as long as anybody cared to listen.

'Mornin', young Luke,' he greeted, his twang as heavily accented as though he'd ridden out of the Alleghenies just the day before. He paused, squinting up at the red eye of the sun. 'Another mild one comin' up by the looks.' Kentucky was contemptuous of the brutal Arizona heat. He contended it never got half as hot here as back home in Kentucky.

To hear him tell it, nothing here was ever anywhere near as hot, cold, beautiful, ugly nor either as good nor as bad as it was back home.

'Yeah, Kentucky,' Luke grinned. 'I got my long johns on.'

The two stood yarning quietly and watching the ranch come to life until the tinkling of the triangle from the house summoned them to breakfast.

The dining room of the Maverick was large and airy with windows opening onto the truck garden in back and well shaded by cottonwoods.

As usual, the two men's places were neatly set out and they could hear Virna bustling about in the kitchen. Tom had at first objected to his wife cooking breakfast after they came home from their honeymoon three years earlier. He had finally relented when he discovered firstly, that his bride was the best cook on the place and, secondly, that she had no intention of allowing him to tell her what she could or could not do in her own home.

A strong-minded woman was Virna Trafford. And pretty as a picture as well, Luke reflected, as she came through the doorway carrying a tin tray laden with platters of bacon and eggs.

'Good morning, Luke, Kentucky,' she smiled, placing the meal on the table. 'Please serve yourselves while I go see what's keeping Tom and Lee.'

She swept out, a slender, straight-backed figure in crisp white muslin with a spotted apron tied about her slender waist.

Kentucky winked as he selected his plate and took a chair.

'So, what do you figure, young Luke? Will it be war or peace over the vittles this morning, you reckon?'

'Let's hope it's peace, old-timer,' Luke responded, taking his place and reaching for the salt. He frowned faintly. Tom and Virna had their small spats like most marrieds, yet he noticed they quarrelled more frequently of late, he wasn't sure why.

Young Lee came in a short time later, his dark hair damped down with water, picking at a blister on his hand.

'Slept in again, boy?' Kentucky grinned around a

mouthful of bacon. 'I declare, the day's going to come when they ain't going to be able to roust you out of that bunk of yours at all.'

'If I looked as old and crinkly as you I'd be happy to stay in bed all day so's I wouldn't frighten folks and scare the stock,' the youth joshed back with a big grin. 'What do you reckon, Luke?

'I say – pass the hominy, Lee,' said Luke. 'Raise a few blisters on the windmill yesterday, did you?'

Lee showed his hands proudly. 'Working like a big dog, Luke.' He sat down and took a platter from the tray. 'Of course that wasn't really good enough for *some* folks I could mention. Even so, I did a tolerable job nonetheless, even if I do say so myself.'

'Well, nobody else is likely to say it,' Kentucky ribbed, then ducked as a chunk of bread came flying his way. 'Bad shooting, boy. Rotten.'

They were laughing as heavy steps sounded and moments later Tom Trafford entered the room, buckling up his belt. 'Private joke or can anybody join in?' he asked.

'Just joshing me about my job of work,' Lee said guardedly.

'Good job,' Tom said. 'But we got another. Some of the shoring in Number Three shaft worked loose yesterday. Reckon the three of us will go take a look at that.'

Luke just nodded in agreement, even though he hated working underground. The brothers had both been reared on the spread but Tom had been able to make the adjustment from rancher to miner with less difficulty than Luke. But Virna's kid brother, Lee, had never adjusted. He'd much rather work for ten bucks a week on the ranch under an open sky than make fifty a day underground.

'Did I hear you say you want Lee to work in the mine today, Tom?' Virna asked, coming in. 'I was hoping he might drive me into Apollo City today to do some shopping.'

Tom Trafford's heavy jaw set, always a sure sign he wasn't pleased.

'There's any number of hands who can drive you, Virna,' he said. 'I need Lee today.'

'But surely any one of a dozen men would be just as good?' Virna countered.

Kentucky quit chewing and and Luke stared at his plate. Storm flags were fluttering. It looked as if today could be a continuation of yesterday, and the day before that.

Tom Trafford swallowed a mouthful and dabbed at his mouth with a napkin. He was boss here and was yet to adjust fully to a strong woman ten years his junior who didn't always hop when he said hop. During their marriage he had found himself obliged to surrender authority in the house to his wife, yet clung stubbornly to the belief that the running of ranch and mine was strictly a man's business.

'Virna,' he stated, 'I've told you before. I'm training Lee to be top-hand on Maverick one day and a man doesn't learn to be best at anything driving ladyfolks into town to shop for play pretties. I'll send Zac with you, or Joe Walsh.'

'Has it ever occurred to you that I might appreciate intelligent company on my journey to and from town, Tom?' she countered. 'I'm sure it has not. I feel quite certain that it never entered your head that if my husband seems unwilling to take me anywhere I might prefer the company of my brother rather than that of a hand?'

'I'm a mighty busy man, Virna,' Tom growled. 'If anybody should know that, it's you. I don't have time for gallivanting.'

Virna flushed. 'So . . . spending a little time with your wife is gallivanting, is it, Tom Trafford? Well, thank you for the compliment.'

'Honey, I didn't mean it that way, honest.'

Too late. A taut silence fell before Lee and Kentucky rose as if on signal.

'Got me a few chores to attend to afore I join the boys, Tom,' Kentucky said, scooping up his hat.

'Want to lend me a hand, Lee?'

Lee glanced uncomfortably at Tom, then nodded to Luke. 'Reckon so. I'll be down to the mine around eight, Tom.'

'Don't be late.'

'No call to say that, Tom,' Luke said mildly. 'If he says he'll be there, he will.'

The wrangle that followed wasn't heated, yet was spirited. It continued for several minutes with first Virna, then Tom seemingly gaining the upper hand. Until Virna finally headed for the doorway, where she paused for a parting shot.

'I'm going to town today. If I can't take one of your precious men with me I shall go by myself. And if I do that I'll set my own time for getting home, which you can be damned well sure will not be early!'

The door banged behind her and big Tom flinched. 'Consarned females. I tell you, Luke, any man would have accepted my explanation just now. I'm running a spread and a mining operation, for God's sake. . . .'

He broke off upon realizing he was talking to himself. His company had abruptly cleared the room and were now visible running for the main gate where a crowd was gathering. He flung his napkin down. 'What now—?'

It didn't take long to find out. By the time he'd joined the swelling crowd, men were to be seen supporting a stranger, a tall, dark-haired man whose chin rested upon his chest, his shirt front soaked in blood. There was something vaguely familiar about the man yet Tom couldn't put his finger on it for a moment.

'Billy Jills found him out on the west graze,' someone said excitedly. 'And Tom, Billy says this here feller says he knows Luke.'

Tom shouldered his way through the growing press of men to get his first clear look at the stranger being supported by several hands.

Immediately, he ordered the man be placed upon the grass. The injured man groaned and rested his head on a waddy's shoulder as they clustered around. He appeared to be around thirty with an athletic build and a face of striking handsomeness despite its pallor.

'How'd he come to git shot?' someone queried, then was pushed aside as Luke Trafford made his way through.

'I don't believe it,' he gasped. 'Clay Grady!'

Every eye switched attention from the injured man to Trafford, for the name of Clay Grady was familiar to every man on Maverick who had ever sat around a campfire listening to Luke Trafford spin tales of his years in uniform in the War Between The States.

'You're sayin' this is your old pard from the Sixth Cavalry, Luke?' Tom said in astonishment.

'Lieutenant Clay Grady,' Luke affirmed, dropping to one knee at the man's side. He drew back the bloodied shirt and saw the bullet wound high up on the chest near the shoulder. 'Clay!' he said loudly. 'Clay, can you hear me?'

'He's not hearin' anything right now, Luke,' Tom pointed out grimly. 'C'mon, fellers, get the man up and get him into the house.'

They didn't respond quickly enough to suit short-fused Tom Trafford, and his voice rose to a shout. 'Move, damnit! You want Luke's pard to croak while you stand about gawking?'

Everybody moved. Fast.

THREE

SECRETS OF THE DESERT

The rancher shrugged. 'Sorry I can't help you none, Sheriff.'

Ben Clanton touched his hatbrim. 'Much obliged for the coffee anyway, Mr Dunbar.'

'The least I could do. Sure hope you run them thieves down.'

'We will, Mr Dunbar, we will,' the lawman replied, as he led his possemen out.

The sheriff of Mercurio sounded reassuring yet his confidence was being slowly but surely eroded by this. He felt drained and bleached out by the blazing sun, and tormented by the hot desert winds.

Five days. . . .

A man on the run could travel vast distances in that stretch of time, he knew. And five days or even less could spell the very limits of endurance for tired and travel-sore townsmen anxious to get back to families and business affairs in town.

The fifteen-man posse rode slowly away from the Harbinger Ranch, raising dust in a sluggish yellow column in its wake. The heat was a massive and elemental force weighing down brutally on men and animals alike. Onwards through sand and rocks they travelled towards the Choctaw Hills, giant saguara cactuses standing sentinel-like wherever the eye fell. This was an arid and brutal stretch of land sprawled beneath the bleached-out dome of the sky.

The sheriff studied hills palpitating in the heat wave, scanning for first sign of his outriding scouts.

The searchers had lost all trace of their quarry's sign in the canyon country late the previous day. The sole reason they had pushed on southward now was the sheriff's instinct. He knew the bank bandits had struck south across the border from Utah and had a hunch they might drive deeper into the wastelands to burn off pursuit.

Clanton glanced back over his shoulder at the

drawn, alkali-dusted faces behind. If that was indeed the outlaws' plan, he reflected, then it might well prove successful. He had serious doubts he'd be able to get these men to saddle up again to take the manhunt any farther south tomorrow.

Cresting a broken-backed ridge they halted to rest their mounts. Staring back at the distant ranchhouse, Clanton noted how tiny and isolated it appeared set against that lonely brown hill behind it with a great empty sweep of nothingness beyond.

The Harbinger was a tiny outpost of life in a harsh land and it took gritty folk to settle here. He reckoned if he had to make a choice, he would rather dodge drunks' bullets in town than be buried alive out here.

They headed on again, the rugged Choctaw Hills drawing slowly nearer by the mile.

Nobody spoke now.

The heat had dried up all attempts at conversation and each man concentrated on merely staying in the saddle and fighting off the smothering heat that tempted them to doze. All but the sheriff himself, that was. Tempered by a life on the hard trails and driven by a sense of duty developed over the years, the lawman drew his strength not from comfort or pleasure but only from success.

An hour later they crossed a series of long dry washes where the sand was deep and made a soft hissing sound against the animals' tired legs.

A mile farther on they sighted the flash of light from the brooding hills.

Clanton immediately called a halt. He figured the flash was likely caused by a chunk of quartz catching the sunlight up there – but it wasn't. He eventually realized the succeeding blinks of light that reached them came from a steel mirror held in a man's hand. He had forward scouts up there, reliable men. 'All right, boys, let's move it along. Looks to me like Charlie and Pete might have struck something.'

The response was discouraging. Even if something had been found up there the horsemen couldn't have cared less by this. The posse largely comprised salesmen, shopkeepers, boozers and bums who straight away started in grumbling and complaining – until the dour lawman wordlessly drew his service revolver and rested it atop the saddle pommel for every man to see.

With another man such action might well be seen as a bluff. Not so with Sheriff Clanton. He meant it as a warning; they knew it, and in no time at all they were making excellent time to put the burning flats behind them then start up the steep hill trail.

Nobody believed the sheriff would actually use a gun to keep possemen in line, but they couldn't be dead certain he might *not* either.

It still took two hours to reach the high ridge where the scouts waited. Charlie Mobbs and Pete Heller were a hardy pair of former buffalo-hunters who eked out a living guiding wagon trains, building fences and occasionally pinning on badges to help out at the law office.

The pair were regarded as troublemakers and hard drinkers in Mercurio. Yet the sheriff never left on a manhunt without them, providing he found them both sober and available. Clanton rated the pair as first-grade scouts second to none and believed his confidence had already been borne out again here today.

He was right, for it turned out the scouts had picked up the outlaws' sign.

Puzzling sign.

Clanton realized this as the scouts guided him around a gaunt ridge to reach the spot where they'd struck pay dirt. It was obvious following a quick inspection that the outlaws had made camp here after crossing the plains. There were scraps of food and cigarette butts, an empty whiskey flask, strange hoofprints. It was plain to see where men had stretched out to rest and footprints led to and from a smooth fat boulder from which they'd maintained a lookout.

All of this seemed straight forward enough. At first. Yet the wide scatter of horse and human tracks beyond the campsite where the horses had been tied up proved puzzling.

Even skilled scouts could not be certain of what had happened here, yet they could make a guess. They speculated that three of the horses could have broken their tethers and made off into the deep draws, while the fourth animal, plainly burdened by a rider, had sped away south in the opposite direction over the hills.

The scouts drew Clanton across to the area where the men they hunted had chased their mounts down afoot. The animals, being well-trained, had plainly not run very far before being recovered, and soon after had been saddled up and also ridden off south, at speed. A quarter-mile from the campsite the possemen came upon a spot where the three horses had plainly overridden the tracks left by the first, effectively blotting them out.

Sweating profusely by this, Clanton hunkered down to study the sign before him patiently with the intensity of a medicine man searching for messages in the elements. He then gazed off south to where rounded hill crests stood etched sharply against the sky. He took out his pipe and stuck it in his mouth without lighting up. He was frowning as he got to speculating out loud: 'Three horses got loose here . . . yet one man gallops off without waiting to help the others round them up. Now why would any man do that to his pards?'

Charlie Mobbs directed a stream of tobacco juice at a curious little lizard which poked its head out of a hole to see what all the uproar was about. The tobacco-spattered head disappeared. Charlie sucked his teeth noisily.

'Iffen a pard done that to me, I wouldn't rate him much of a friend, Sheriff,' he drawled. He spat again. 'No siree, Ben, I sure enough wouldn't be doin' that.'

'And what sort of dumb outlaw would be careless enough not to secure his cayuse when he was on the run from the John Laws, anyways?' speculated Pete Heller. He squinted narrowly at the lawman. 'Somethin' mighty odd here. But if I had to bet hard money, Sheriff, I'd hazard a guess that these here badmen had themselves a fallin' out. It wouldn't surprise me none if one of 'em elected to hightail it, and scattered his pards' hosses so as to give himself a good head start.'

Clanton considered this pensively for a long moment, then uncoiled to his feet. Today, he was totally ignoring stiff joints and saddle chafe. 'And taking your notion another step ahead, Pete, it just could be that the first rider took something with him. Right?'

'The dinero, you figure, Sheriff?'

'That would be my best guess.'

The bunch fell silent for a time after that, each man envisioning a possible falling-out among thieves. And the longer the sheriff pondered, the more sense this notion seemed to make to him. He knew the badman breed inside and out. Honour amongst such men was rare. They lived not by principle but by the law of the quick – the knife in the back, the bullet from the dark – and the devil take the hindmost!

At last he spoke. 'What lies beyond these hills, boys?'

'Lizard Desert,' Mobbs supplied. 'Ranch country west, badlands east. If you keep pushin' south far enough you come to the Capitans.'

'Tough country?'

'The toughest.'

Clanton nodded, 'Let's get back to the men.'

'Men?' Heller sneered as they started down. 'Look more like a bunch of frazzled old ladies to me, Sheriff. Could be you're goin' to find it hard to get 'em started up again now.'

The lawman looked the bunch over when they got back. Every man was sprawled out motionless in what little shade was offered. Only a few made the effort to sit up lethargically when informed of what had been found, and right after that he issued orders to mount up.

Nobody moved. Not one man. If any man was energized to hear that the lost sign had been picked up again, he did a masterful job of concealing it.

'We've been talkin', Sheriff,' the storekeeper said at length. 'We've had enough.'

'More'n enough,' supported another. 'We can't make it another mile. And we ain't a-gonna even try, by God!'

The two were quickly proven wrong on both counts when the lawman dropped hand on gunbutt and ordered them into their saddles or face the consequences, before once more leading them out.

But progress proved painfully slow, so much so that within a few miles Clanton was forced to offer a reluctant compromise. He agreed that should contact with their quarry not be made by noon the following day he would abandon the chase and permit them to return home.

Holding his mount back until the last rider had moved out ahead of him, Clanton was about to follow when he took one last glance out across the plains and glimpsed a tiny column of dust climbing the sky far back in the direction of the Harbinger spread.

With a frown he drew a set of battered old army field glasses from his saddlebag. Adjusting the screws to bring the dust cloud into focus, he picked out two horsemen leading a laden pack animal.

'What've we got, Sheriff?' Pete Heller called from higher up the slope.

Clanton lowered the glasses slowly. 'Two men. Can't see who they are from here, but I reckon I can have an educated guess.'

Heller spat. 'Bounty hunters?'

With a nod, Clanton replaced the glasses and heeled his prad upslope. Bounty hunters was his guess, sure enough. Human bloodhounds. Men who hunted outlaws, not to bring them to justice but for the cash money they would fetch, alive or dead. They were a breed he thoroughly detested.

And yet he realized it was inevitable that the robbery of the Mercurio Bank should attract such men, for Banker Dolan had already posted a $1,000 reward on the robbers' heads plus a quarter share of all money recovered as an added incentive.

Should any bounty hunter capture both the bandits and the plunder, his reward would amount to some $3,500. He knew several in the bunch who'd track down their own mothers for far less than that.

The sun seemed to flood down with heightened ferocity upon the wide reaches of Lizard Desert south of the Sawbucks as they travelled. Even the leathery sheriff was sagging in his saddle by the time they reached the desert floor several hours later. And what was to be found there did nothing to uplift sagging spirits. While they'd been riding, the desert winds had been industriously busy, sweeping and cleaning up like a conscientious housewife at the end of the day.

No sign worth a damn to be sighted in any direction now.

While the men rested up from a combination of fatigue and disappointment, Clanton and his scouts fanned out wide in search of sign – any sign would do. But by sundown the only tracks to be sighted on this bleak yellow sector of Lizard Desert were their own.

Ben Clanton felt double his forty-five years as they set off through the rapidly chilling twilight to rejoin the main bunch and instruct them to head on home. For a moment the lawman was tempted to ride back with them. But the moment quickly passed. He knew that morning would find him, stubborn and dogged, pushing south again either alone or in the company of Mobbs and Heller. Quitting was not a word in the sheriff of Mercurio's dictionary.

FOUR

HARD MILES SOUTH

Virna emerged from the sick room carrying a bloodstained shirt, a dish of water and a bottle of laudanum. Tom and Luke Trafford turned from the windows, each with the same question in his eyes.

'I expect he will be all right now,' she said. She held up the porcelain dish that contained knife, forceps, and a flattened .45 slug. 'The bullet was easy to remove. It had barely broken the skin where it came through beneath the armpit. He's weak from blood loss, of course, but he should be fine in a day or two.'

'You're plain amazing, honey,' Tom enthused,

squeezing her shoulders. 'Luke, have I ever told you just how many sterling qualities this girl has?'

Luke nodded. He was pleased to see the couple back on good terms again. Yet at the moment he was far more interested in the wounded man.

'I still reckon we should send to Apollo City for Doc Speers, Virna,' he opined.

'Of course that would be the sensible thing, Luke,' she said. 'But the patient won't hear of it.'

'No surprise there. He always mistrusted medics during the war,' Luke said with a rueful grin. 'Medics, officers, politicians . . . I doubt he even trusted our own leaders. Can I see him?'

'For a short time only, Luke. We mustn't tire him out. You'll see Luke doesn't stay too long, won't you, Tom? I reckon those two are just dying to start in reliving the old days, but that will have to wait until later.'

'I'll see to it, honey,' Tom replied. He turned to Luke. 'I reckon I'm as curious as you to find out what happened to your old war buddy, Luke.'

'Who isn't?' Luke replied. 'Thanks, Virna, for your help,' he added, then led the way into the room.

Virna had drawn the bedroom shades against the glare. Clayton Grady lay in the big double bed propped up on two plump pillows. He was stripped to the waist with heavy, white bandaging across his chest and around the left shoulder. Contrasting with his coal-black hair, the wounded man's face was pale and gaunt-looking, but the grin he put on as they entered took Luke back to bygone days when Clay Grady's careless smile had been as familiar and unchanging as the scream of shells or the stink of death.

'Gents,' Grady said. 'That is some nursemaid you have yourselves here. Makes it almost worthwhile getting shot. You're a real lucky *hombre*, Tom.'

'I know it,' Tom replied. 'So, how does it feel now?'

'Better without that slug, let me assure you. This is wild country you live in down here, Luke.'

Luke rested crossed arms on the end of the big brass bed. 'What happened to you, Clay?'

'Damndest thing,' Grady answered in his clipped, well-educated way. 'I was working over in Nevada when I heard you were living over here on the Maverick. So naturally I packed my playing cards and my best shirt and headed your way – fast.'

'But how'd you get shot?'

This drew a frown.

'Damndest thing. When dark caught up with me out at Rogue River I elected to camp and make a fresh start next morning. Then just as I was near asleep, in came these camp-robbers. I braced the bastards and next thing lead was flying all over. Reckon I winged a couple while getting to my horse, but they were still throwing lead. Cut the horse down and clipped me ... sons of bitches. They came on after me but I stood them off until they decided they'd had enough and hightailed it. So I started making on for the spread ... and I guess I don't recollect much more of anything.'

'Damndest thing, like you say,' Tom said soberly. 'I don't recollect any trouble like this hereabouts in a coon's age. I'll report it to the sheriff right away.'

'Forget it, Tom,' Grady grinned. 'I'm a high-roller and travel in style. My horse was worth five hundred bucks. A man rides tall, he's got to expect to attract a little trouble.' He winked at Luke. 'So, I guess this old leopard hasn't changed its spots, eh, pard?'

'He had more ways of getting in and out of trouble in the war than any ten men, Tom,' Luke admitted ruefully to the others. 'But Tom's right, Clay. We should report this.'

'I'd sooner you didn't, man,' Grady said, sober now. He studied both men in silence for a long moment before he went on. 'To be truthful, I'd prefer it if word didn't get around that I'm visiting you folks. Now I know that might sound curious, but I can explain. When I quit Nevada it was what you might call a strategic withdrawal. There was a man there, a fat cattleman with a lot of money and a beautiful daughter. . . . Er, need I go on, Luke?'

Luke laughed. 'Same old Clay. No, you don't have to say any more, man. Tom, you're looking at a *hombre* who could just never stay away from a high-stake poker game . . . or keep a pretty woman at arm's length.'

'Now, don't exaggerate my shortcomings, Luke,' Grady laughed.

'Not much chance of that, Clay,' Tom said. 'Luke's talked some about you since he came home from the wars. We know you were a fine soldier and we're mighty proud to have you come stay with us to make up for the hard time you had getting here.'

'Why, that's a mighty pleasing thing to hear, Tom,' Grady said warmly. 'But I feel kind of embarrassed about all this. I planned to arrive here in style. I mean, when you haven't sighted an old pard in years, the least a man can do is arrive with a bit of a flourish.'

Everybody grinned, but the smiles faded fast when the patient began to cough.

'Looks like we'd better let you get some rest,' Tom said. 'C'mon, Luke. I'll send Virna back in to check you out, Clay.'

'Much obliged, pard.' Grady coughed then winked at Luke. 'I reckon I'll need to be at full strength when we get down to spinning old lies about what heroes we were in those days, man.'

'I was the hero – you just made up the numbers,' Luke grinned, making for the door. He paused, sobering. 'Now all you've got to do is rest up easy, hear?'

'Easy it'll be.'

The brothers went out to find Lee waiting in the passageway. 'What are you doing here, boy?' Tom said gruffly. 'You're supposerd to be working at the mine.'

'Just had to find out if your friend's all right, Luke,' Lee said. 'Is he?'

'Reckon he is, Lee,' Luke replied. 'Always was a hard man to hurt.'

'Will he be staying on?'

'Reckon so.'

'How'd he come to get shot up like this, Luke?' the boy asked, but Tom cut him off.

'You'll get all the news over supper, Lee. C'mon, we'll go see Virna, then get along to the mine. Luke, you'd better stay close around here in case you're needed.'

'Right,' Luke agreed. 'I'll go tend to some chores

at the stables. You can tell Virna where I am in case she needs me.'

He started off across the gallery and went down the steps. He paused momentarily to glance back at the bedroom window, then strode on across the wide yard, shaking his head and grinning. He still couldn't quite believe it. Though they'd been pards during a brief part of the war, he'd never really expected to run into Clay Grady afterwards. He'd always intended to return to ranching, while Grady, as he'd so often stated during the war, meant to return to his old way of life as well. In his case, that meant lovely women, high-stake gambling and what he vaguely termed as 'foot-loosing'.

He felt flattered that Grady would seek him out after all those years, for although thrown together in the army they had always been very different breeds of men. He remembered often feeling stodgy and dull in Grady's mercurial company, and doubtless would get to feel that way again.

And knew he would enjoy every moment of it.

Kentucky met him at the stable doors. The old-timer was curious to hear all about Grady, so Luke kept talking while he worked about the stables for some time before he realized Kentucky appeared to have become strangely sober and thoughtful.

'What's the matter, old-timer? You look like

you're chewing on something you don't quite like the taste of.'

'Nothin' botherin' me, Luke.'

'Sure there is. I know you too well. What's on your mind? Has it something to do with Clay?'

Grunting, Kentucky hoisted a saddle, rested it on a tree, then set about working on it with brush and saddle soap.

'Well, mebbe I'm old and crochetty and a kinda suspicious old swayback about some things, boy, but—'

'There's no maybe about that,' Luke broke in. 'Those are about the kindest things folks say about you. But quit blowing on the fur and get to the hide, old-timer. What's really sticking in your craw?'

Kentucky rubbed the saddle vigorously.

'Well, this feller says he was jumped out by Rogue River and walked here to the spread, right?'

'Right.'

'So, how come he was coated in alkali? And how come there's salt dust on his saddle like he'd been out in the desert?'

'There's odd patches of desert between the Rogue and the Nevada border, Kentucky.'

'Yeah, but not this side. Seems to me from what I see of your pard, he's a bit of a dude. I just can't see him sleeping rough and dirty. I'd expect a stylish pilgrim like that to wash up real good after crossing desert country. Wouldn't you?'

Luke stopped working.

'You know, you just about beat all, you old varmint. I swear you must be the most mistrustful *hombre* in Arizona. Small wonder they booted you out of Kentucky.'

'I was just remarkin'. Seems curious to me, is all. And then there's the saddle.'

'What about the saddle?'

'A man gets shot up fifteen miles away, loses his hoss, yet totes a big heavy saddle with him. Does that make any sort of sense to you? No, it don't. And it makes even less sense when the saddle ain't worth a cuss.'

'How do you know it isn't?'

By way of reply, Kentucky went through to the tackroom and returned toting a flashy black leather saddle. Turning it upside down, he revealed the padding missing, the lining torn and soiled.

'So?' Luke growled. 'Maybe it has sentimental value?' He grinned suddenly. 'Or maybe his mother rode it during Pickett's Charge at Gettysburg. Then again, he could have brought it along with him here just because he knew there could be some nosey old cracker like you who'd give himself a headache trying to figure out why he took the trouble to carry it with him.'

Kentucky placed the battered saddle upon the tree and stared at it thoughtfully. Then he said quietly, 'You think right high of this feller, don't you, young Luke?'

'Sure. And with good reason. Clay Grady's a good man, Kentucky. And everything I said about what he did in the war, is true. I'm right proud to call him a friend.'

'In that case . . . I'd best keep my mouth shut.' Kentucky winked as he toted the saddle back out to the tackroom. 'How many times have you told me I talk far too much, anyway?'

'Who can count that high?' Luke retorted.

It ended there. Luke didn't give the older man's words a second thought, for it was a fact of life on Maverick that Kentucky was naturally sceptical of just about everything and everybody.

The two discussed Clay Grady and the war as they worked, and Kentucky seemed his usual easy-going self by the time Luke finally quit the stables to return to the house and check on his patient.

He found Grady still sleeping and Virna hustling about the big airy kitchen boiling bandaging and sterilizing utensils. She fixed him a mug of coffee and they chatted about Clay as she continued with her chores. Tom came in later and Virna welcomed him with a kiss and poured more coffee, and it did Luke good to see them back on good terms again.

As he rolled and lighted a cigarette he glanced in the direction of Clay's room, nodded to himself. That was it, he mused. Life had been getting too humdrum and predictable on the Maverick of late. The dramatic arrival of Clay Grady had shaken things up and it was possible now that Tom mightn't be so preoccupied with work from here on, nor Virna as resentful of the feeling that she was being taken for granted.

He hoped that proved to be the case.

The more he thought about things the more sure he felt that Grady's arrival would prove a good thing, not only for him but for everybody.

'More coffee, Luke?'

'Why not, Virna? I've had two mugs, so a third can't do much more harm.'

'I'll take a mug in and go see if Clay's awake yet if you like, Virna?' Tom offered.

'All right, darling. But get me the whiskey first. He told me he only ever takes coffee with whiskey added.'

Luke laughed softly as Tom rose and went to the liquor cabinet. 'Same old Clay,' he murmured. 'That man hasn't changed one bit.'

The pale light in the east slowly changed into a strong glow behind the distant hills. Then it became golden as the sun appeared, opening slowly like the lid of an eye to gaze down upon the campsite where the bounty hunters slept.

A chill breeze snaked from the jaws of a canyon and stirred the cold campfire, dusting the blanket-shrouded figures with ashes.

McCoy sneezed in his sleep and promptly awakened. He sat up like a grizzly bear aroused from hibernation to stare blearily around at a world that seemed not even remotely to his liking.

Scratching his rough black thatch, McCoy turned morosely to stare across at his sleeping partner. He was envious of Mallone's ability to sleep late. He'd been a late sleeper himself once, but five years in the Utah Territorial Penitentiary where they rousted you out at five o'clock, winter and summer, had cured him of that luxurious habit for life.

Sometimes McCoy dreamed the penitentiary was burning to the ground taking inmates and custodians alike to a fiery eternity.

This was a good dream.

But more frequently he dreamed of living high on the hog with whiskey that never ceased to flow, tobacco that tasted good enough to eat, and a fat and willing woman always within easy reach. That dream was infinitely better.

'Get up!' he growled, lumbering erect. 'Half the day gone already and not a hand's turn done.' Built like a barrel and as big as a bear, two-fisted McCoy was never at his best in the early hours of any new day.

Mallone continued to snore despite repeated admonitions to rise until the fragrance of sizzling bacon and boiling coffee finally freed him from the arms of Morpheus. The lean gunpacker awoke refreshed. No dreams either pleasant or otherwise ever disturbed Mallone's nights.

'Hot one by the looks, pard,' he commented, finger-combing his hair.

McCoy gulped scalding coffee and jabbed at the bacon with a stick. 'It's hot and it's late.'

'So, what's the hurry? We don't have no sign to follow.'

It was still too early for McCoy to come fully to grips with reality. But his partner had confronted him with it, ready or not. For not only had they failed to find any trace of the outlaws but the desert winds had also erased the signs of the sheriff and the two scouts which they had followed unseen into the Lizard the previous day.

The prospect of $1,000 bounty money, or maybe even more if they recovered some or all of the stolen money, was fading fast.

'Eat,' McCoy grumped.

Mallone ate.

Both men shovelled their chow into their mouths with their fingers, packing bread in on top of it and washing it all down with hot joe. The desert's night cold continued to linger in the shadows but the sun was already beginning to warm them now. The stiffness of sleep gradually left McCoy's face as food did its healing work. Tossing his tin plate aside the big man lighted a cigar and tugged out a whiskey flask. Several slugs, a few puffs, and this bounty man was ready for the trail again.

He tossed the flask across to his partner and belched greasily.

'We got two choices as I see it, Mallone. We can ride around out here like idiots, or quit and head for town and get drunk.'

Mallone swigged, liked the taste, took another pull. He corked the bottle and stood it upright in the sand. 'Clanton ain't quittin',' he said.

'The man's a mule. Ain't human.'

'Smarter than that. Four men. Four men and ten thousand dollars in cash money. Ain't no way a big-dinero party that size can just up and disappear. Sooner or later they got to bob up someplace.'

'And how would we know them if they did? We

56

don't even have names for this bunch. Four masked jokers knock over a bank. Two tall, two short. That's all we know. Hell, they could buy us a drink and we still wouldn't even know!'

Mallone hoisted the whiskey bottle. 'Rotgut!' he said morosely. He tossed it to McCoy. 'Cheapest you can buy. How long since we could afford a bottle of real, honest-to-God sippin' whiskey?'

'What's that got to do with anything'?'

Mallone's eyes glittered. He was a dangerous man. 'It means if we quit this here manhunt we will go on drinkin' swill. Hell, could be in time we might even have to go to work!'

Work! The dreaded word. Yet suddenly McCoy appeared purposeful as he got to his feet. 'Could be I was talkin' hasty, Mallone.' He hazarded a grin. 'Maybe I could stand to lose a little back fat if it came to that. . . .'

Mallone beamed in response as he scrambled to his feet. McCoy mightn't be much of a partner but he was all he had.

'I sure am partial to fine sippin' whiskey, McCoy. So . . . let's get to work!'

FIVE

THE HARD MILES SOUTH

Standing guard on the gold room near the adit of Maverick Mine, ranch hand Conway Lewis could hear Tom Trafford chiding the youth as he emerged from the shaft.

'If you'd put that chock into the chute like I told you to, boy, the damned thing wouldn't have come apart on us when we loaded.'

'I put it there, Tom,' came Lee's response. 'You just never told me to hammer it in hard, so I didn't.'

'Do I have to tell you every damn thing?'

Tom was peevish as they emerged into the bright sunlight. He was strippped to the waist and sweating freely, big muscular torso gleaming. Crossing to Lewis, he snapped his fingers, and the man quickly handed him a swab of cotton waste. He stood wiping the sweat off his chest and glowering at the boy.

Lee glanced at Lewis appealingly, and the man felt a twinge of sympathy. He might have spoken up for the kid if he'd had the nerve, but settled for just a reassuring grin.

'Somethin' amusing you?' Trafford barked.

Lewis's smile vanished. 'Huh? Hell no, Tom, nothing at all.'

'It just could be this sentry job is too soft for you, mister. Maybe I'll have Luke hand you a pick and shovel tomorrow.'

He seemed to expect some response. But Conway Lewis was too shrewd for that. Disappointed, Trafford plucked his shirt from a post and went striding off toward the three men working the stamp mill crushing ore. Lewis cocked an eyebrow at Lee.

'His bark's worse than his bite, kid.'

'He can go to hell,' Lee said. He glanced toward the house where he could see a tall, dark-haired figure seated in a rocker on the front gallery. 'He can fix that damned chute himself. I'm going up to talk with Clay.'

'Big Tom mightn't care for that.'

'I said he can go to hell. I've done a full day's work. Anyway, Clay can likely use a little company.'

'Could be. Although I've seen Mrs Trafford fussin' about him all afternoon.'

'Well, he's a man worth fussing over. Clay appreciates what you do for him. Not like some people.'

'You think a lot of Grady, don't you, Lee?'

'Doesn't everybody?'

'You got somethin' there. Right decent feller, he is, even if a bit of a dude . . . and a mystery, I guess. Good to see him back on his feet again, ain't it?'

'Sure enough. I can tell you that if it wasn't for Luke and Clay I'd be thinkin' of packing my warbag.'

'That's loco talk, Lee. I known Tom Trafford. He thinks a heap of you.'

'Who cares?'

Lee spun on his heel and headed off up the slope past the crusher, shoulders defiantly stiff. Lewis saw Trafford glance after the boy but didn't attempt to stop him. Tom likely realized he'd been rough on the youngster, Lewis guessed. Then he saw Grady smile a welcome to the boy and just a short time later Virna Trafford appeared on the veranda with a pitcher of cold lemonade.

Lewis watched the little group for some minutes before glancing across at the crusher to see Tom Trafford also watching them.

It seemed to Lewis that the boss had a grouchy set to his jaw as he returned to his chores.

At sundown Luke Trafford rode in from the range, left his horse at the stables and walked on down to the mine. The lamps had just been lit and the door to the gold room stood open. He could see his brother inside frowning down at the tally sheet in his hands.

Luke nodded to Conway Lewis and entered the chamber. Tom glanced up, then returned his attention to the sheet.

'We're behind schedule,' was his greeting.

Lowering himself onto an empty crate, Luke fingered his hat back from his forehead to let his eyes play over the shelves containing the fat little canvas sacks that contained the mine's production over almost three months.

He was weary from a long day out on the range and the sight of his brother still hard at work made him feel even wearier.

'We've had more than our usual number of hold-ups and delays this month, Tom,' he pointed out. 'You know that.'

'We're still behind schedule for the shipping date,' came the terse reply. 'Know what I think? I reckon the seams are playin' out. We're workin' just as hard but not gettin' the gold.'

'Well, the assay agent told us the seam was never all that deep. We've always known the mine would peter out sooner or later.'

'And you don't give a cuss, do you? Don't bother to deny it, Luke. I know you hate the mine and always have.'

'Seems to me we were all doing fine here before we struck gold.'

'We were poor, mister.'

'There's worse things than being poor.'

'Like what?'

'Well, like working like a dog and expecting everyone else to do the same, for instance. What's eating you today anyway, Tom? I thought you were starting to relax some last week. But now you're going at it harder then ever.'

'I'll relax after we ship to Phoenix.'

'Wrong,' Luke replied, rising. He plucked the tally sheet from his brother's fingers and tossed it aside. 'You're through for the day. Right now, you're going up to the house to set on the gallery and relax until supper. Virna told me she's fixing roast ribs for tonight.'

Tom's jaw shot out. 'You're maybe bossin' this outfit now, mister?'

'Just for tonight I sure am.' Luke gestured at the door. 'Move!'

Abruptly, Tom Trafford's face split into a broad grin, that old easy smile that was a rare thing around Maverick these days. He threw an arm around his brother's shoulders and together they walked out. 'Lock her up, Conway,' he ordered as they passed by the sentry. 'And when the night guard takes over come on up to the house and have a drink with us.'

'Huh? Oh . . . yeah, sure,' Lewis said, surprised.

'Wear your drinking shirt, Conway,' Luke called back. 'You never know, we just all might get drunk tonight.'

'No "might" about it,' Tom laughed, and suddenly thrusting Luke aside, began to run for the house. 'Come on, Luke, race you up if you ain't too old and creaky!'

Conway Lewis smiled broadly as he watched them tearing up the yard like a pair of schoolboys. This was more like it, he thought. This was more like the old days before Tom Trafford had begun to change.

Clayton Grady sighed. 'An exquisite meal. And if I might make so bold as to say so – prepared by an exquisitely lovely lady. What do you say, Tom?'

'Took the words right out of my mouth, Clay,' Tom smiled from his end of the table. 'Luke, pass around the cigars.'

'I'll skip the cigars,' Virna smiled as she rose.

Grady rose and didn't resume his seat until she had left the table.

Pausing in the doorway, Virna looked back, her expression wistful. If only Tom would say things like that just now and again, she mused. If only he would stand up when she left the room the way he had done when they were first married.

She cut off that line of thought quickly, feeling guilty now. She shouldn't be critical, she chided herself. Particularly not tonight when Tom seemed in such an unusually light-hearted mood. She turned away and as she entered the kitchen to fix the coffee, heard Clay Grady's cultivated voice say:

'You're a mighty lucky man, Tom Trafford . . . or maybe I've already told you that?'

'Disreputable' was the definitive term for Charlie Mobbs and Pete Heller at the best of times, and the spectacle the pair presented when in the grip of crippling hangovers could be something to see. To Sheriff Ben Clanton, his scouts looked like something the dogs had had under the house as they rode into his camp in the Capitan foothills that morning to say goodbye. Not that he blamed them for tying one on in Yellow River. Mobbs and Heller were hardcases but were also highly professional at their work and didn't tolerate failure any better than he did. They'd earned a blow-out, but like always, had overdone it.

'Of course, we'd be willing to stay on with you iffen there was any point, Sheriff,' Mobbs offered, shaking hands with trembling fingers.

'No point now, Charlie,' Clanton said. 'If I come up with anything now it'd only be dumb luck.' He shook hands with Heller whose complexion had a vaguely greenish tinge. 'You've been a great help to me, boys, like always. But you get yourselves on back to Mercurio now.'

Mobbs managed to mount up without much difficulty but his partner was compelled to lead his horse off to a boulder to enable him to fill his saddle.

The lawman's smile quickly faded as he watched the pair ride off slowly into the hills. It was difficult to remember just how long ago it was since he had ridden from Mercurio with seven good men. Now he was alone.

At last he turned back to the camp, doused the fire and prepared for the trail. The previous day he had visited three foothill villages and spoken to the lawmen there without success. If the bank thieves had made it all the way south to the Capitans, then it seemed they'd succeeded in passing through undetected.

Yet Clanton refused to believe that four men with ten thousand dollars could have made the arduous desert journey then faced up to the even more testing moutain crossing without having to stop off some place for supplies. Yet nobody seemed to have sighted them.

The alternative facing him was intimidating. It suggested the outlaws had branched off on the way south, and whether they'd gone east or west he had no way of guessing. In his mind's eye he visualized vast tracts of country on either side of the southward route – badlands to the east and endless rangelands to the west.

An impossibly massive area for one man to search.

Yet as he swung up to head off slowly across the plain with the mighty bulk of the Capitans at his back, the lawman set about narrowing down the possibilities in his mind. Instinct told him the outlaws would not have entered the badlands unless they'd been hard-pushed and desperate. But had they done so, he doubted he could expect to run them down alone. That would be a task for an army.

This only left the range country west of Lizard Desert. He was unfamiliar with that region but his scouts had informed that it was dotted with ranches and towns, some of the latter quite sizable.

So, where might four badmen with big money to spend be likely to head to rest up?

Of course there would be a certain anonymity to be had in large towns, yet there was also the danger of the local lawmen who might get suspicious about strangers with big money. If the hellions were really smart they might instead try to get ranch jobs and wait for things to cool down before making a splash with their new wealth, or maybe striking off to Mexico or California.

Indications were that his quarry were smart enough. They had plundered the Mercurio bank expertly and had proven clever enough to elude his pursuit ever since.

He eventually decided to go check out the towns while not overlooking the ranches, the bigger outfits in particular.

He rode steadily north-west over the plain, a solitary horseman kicking dust into a brassy sky.

'And then,' Clay Grady said soberly, 'there was Shiloh. . . .'

'Shiloh,' Luke Trafford echoed. 'Now Shiloh was somethin' I wouldn't care to live through again. . . .'

'Confederates pounding the daylights out of us on two sides and Stonewall Jackson up front with the good Lord alone knew how many regiments . . . and not one man of us brave enough to admit how scared he was. . . .'

Their audience sat enthralled as late Sunday afternoon shadows dappled the long front veranda of the Maverick ranch house – Tom, Kentucky, Virna and a wide-eyed young Lee Clarke.

The stories the veterans were spinning conjured up images of the massive, brutal sweep of it all, the deeds of great bravery and of craven cowardice, good generals and bad, endless weeks of inactivity wedged in between mighty battle actions and the brutal, seemingly endless months of day-to-day fighting.

None could deny that the Civil War had written the darkest pages of American history. Yet the way Luke and Clay told it, the glory also came alive, leavened with humor and illuminated by the modesty of two veterans who refused to portray themselves as heroes but rather as observers caught up in history in the making.

Grady did most of the talking. He was a natural story spinner and obviously loved an audience. His recovery from the gunshot wound was almost complete by this and he made a striking figure as he lounged gracefully in a deep chair, dressed in one of Tom's good shirts that was several sizes too large plus a pair of Luke's brown twill pants. Puffing on a cigar, he was the picture of a man totally at ease with the world and the company he shared.

It was only when Virna announced that it was time to think about supper, that the afternoon's reminiscing drew to a close.

'There's a couple of things I need to attend to down at the mine,' Tom announced, getting to his feet. 'Want to lend me a hand, Luke?'

'Surely it can wait until tomorrow, Tom?' Virna asked. 'Why not stay here with Clay until supper is ready?'

'It won't take long,' Tom replied, descending the steps. 'Comin', Luke?'

Luke rose reluctantly. 'Seems I'm tuckered out by all the fighting we've been doing,' he joked. 'But, yeah, I'm coming.'

'Maybe I can help?' offered Grady. He thumped his chest. 'Strong as a bull now – if you'll pardon the expression, Virna?'

'You need to be at least that strong to survive around this spread,' Luke smiled, going down the steps. 'And you're not quite there no matter what you think.' He winked. 'So just stay put. We're not having any relapses.'

'Salt of the earth, that man,' Grady murmured, watching the brothers' tall figures recede. 'Luke would hate to hear me say it, but you know he was about the bravest man I ever clapped eyes on in the war.'

Lee said, 'Luke says the same about you, Clay.'

'He would,' Grady replied. 'Even if it was a lie. The truth is, he spent as much time getting me out of one scrape or another as he did fighting the enemy.'

'Would you care for a drink before I start supper, Clay?' asked Virna. 'Coffee, perhaps?'

She was standing by his chair. Grady studied her through a film of cigar smoke. Her thick hair rippled to her shoulders and her lighty tanned complexion made her teeth appear very white. She was dressed in a cambric blouse and vividly-patterned Mexican skirt with a sash at the waist.

He rose and smiled.

'I'm fine thanks, Virna. And, like I've said before, you can stop fussing over me now. Not that I haven't enjoyed every minute of it, of course.'

She flushed, smiled, and turned away. 'Come on, Lee. I can use some help.'

'Do I have to, Virna?'

'Yes, you do. Kentucky can keep Clay company. Come along.'

Resuming his seat as the two went inside, Grady reached for the cigars again. Kentucky sat on the top step, brushing a cleaning rag along the barrel of his long rifle. The old man glanced up, watching Grady light the cigar.

'You sure have led an exciting life, young feller,' he commented.

'It likely sounds that way in the telling, Kentucky. But I've had plenty ups and downs, dull spots too.'

'Guess you found life quiet after Appomattox?'

'At times,' Grady said guardedly. 'Why do you ask?'

'Just curious, I guess. Seems I ain't heard you say nothin' on what you been doing since the war.'

'No mystery, old-timer. I've been what you'd call a drifter. California after gold, Montana with cattle, gambling on the riverboats out of New Orleans. You name it and I've most likely done it.'

'That suits you then? The drifter's life?'

'Like a glove. But you seem sceptical, Kentucky. Why so?'

Kentucky focused upon his rifle.

'Oh, I guess it just struck me that a feller with your style and education might want more out of life. You seem to have a taste for good whiskey, fine clothes, all that sort of thing. And Luke just happened to mention that when you were in the army together, most all you ever talked about was makin' it real big when the war was over.'

Kentucky paused to look up with a shrewd expression seaming his face. 'Guess you dropped that notion some place, huh?'

'Guess I did at that,' Grady said quietly, showing the first sign of weariness. He was well aware that while everyone else on the Maverick seemed to accept him unquestioningly as Luke's wartime pard, the leathery old-timer might have some reservations.

There were times when he would glance up suddenly to find Kentucky's gaze fixed upon him as though attempting to see right through him. It might be risky to dismiss this old cracker too lightly, he warned himself. He felt secure in his situation here on the Maverick thus far but realized it might be unwise to get complacent.

'Nice rifle that, Kentucky,' he remarked after a silence, deliberately changing the subject.

'Old like me,' Kentucky grunted noncommittally, getting up. 'Well, best I was gettin' down to the bunkhouse to wash up. That Virna can be right brisk when it comes to throwin' a mess of vittles together.' He started down the steps, paused. 'So, reckon you'll be stayin' on with us a spell, young feller?'

'Drifters never make plans, old-timer.'

'Uh-huh,' Kentucky grunted and went off with the long rifle cradled in the crook of his arm leaving a suddenly uneasy Clay Grady staring after him.

And he thought, 'Smart or just nosy?' Then admitted he couldn't decide which.

The chair creaked as he rose. He paced the long gallery, an easy-striding man, smooth as glass. Pausing at the far end he stared eastward across the dusk-shrouded range. Beyond the spread's boundaries lay the desert and its dead. He felt certain his three enemies had been killed. Which only left the law to worry about. And with so much time elapsing since the shooting, he doubted that factor would prove of any concern now.

He was smiling a strange smile as he turned to retrace his steps. Behind his smile the true Clayton Grady was aware that time was running out. He was the guest of honor here because of his wartime friendship with Luke, no other reason. But there was a limit to how long that situation might last. Sooner or later the past and his real nature could betray him – and there was always a risk Luke might somehow get to realize that the only reason he'd acquitted himself so well during the war was that he was a man who loved to kill.

Since Appomattox, Clayton Grady had returned to type. That meant dead men behind him, Wanted dodgers, bounty hunters eager to claim the reward money posted on him in other places.

He nodded. Yeah, time and luck had to be running out on him about now. He would disappear soon and they would never know which way he'd gone.

Him and the gold. . . .

SIX

ALONG CAME A LAWMAN

No doubt about it, Grady told himself. The longer he was here the more he appreciated the stroke of inspiration that had seen him make his way to Luke Trafford's spread that wild night.

Of course he would likely have been able to lie convincingly enough to save himself even had he landed among total strangers. But it was good to feel safe and secure here . . . really good.

Good old Luke.

Yet that thought caused his mood to change abruptly, and there was a hint of contempt in his face now as he muttered aloud, 'Good old *trusting* Luke!'

Luke had trusted him right from the get-go, he mused, lighting up. The man needed to be like that to ignore the many allegations of corruption and violence that had marked Clay Grady's army service. More often than not his superiors had turned a blind eye to Grady's indiscretions simply to keep a superb fighting soldier out of the brig and in the front line where he belonged. And not even Clay Grady's many enemies could deny he'd been a highly accomplished killer of Johnny Rebs.

He doubted Luke had ever suspected that the reason behind his lethal expertise was his hunger to kill. His wartime pard simply didn't think that way. Grady had saved Trafford's life on several occasions, and that in itself ensured his blindness to any faults Grady might have.

He paused by the steps.

Kentucky was over by the cookshack yarning with two cowhands. That old-timer had displayed some curiosity about how he'd spent the time since war's end, Grady reflected thoughtfully.

Then he grinned. He wondered how folks here would react were they to learn that three of those years had been spent behind the high walls of Yuma Penitentiary, with most of his otherwise free time taken up with riding the owlhoot in a dozen states and territories under aliases.

Maybe that canny old Kentucky wouldn't be all that surprised to hear the truth about his past, he conceded. But, of course, Luke would be stunned, disbelieving. His war buddy Clayton Grady of the Fighting Sixth a bloody outlaw? Impossible!

He chuckled at the thought. But he sobered to ponder briefly on how long he might stay on, keeping in mind this was likely the safest possible place for him for the time being.

'Clay!'

He swung at the sound of Virna's voice to see her leaning from a window.

'Supper will be ready in just a few minutes,' she smiled.

'Much obliged,' he drawled. 'I'll go spruce up some.'

The woman vanished and Grady stood stroking his jaw, conscious of an old familiar stirring. He loved women and by nature tended to grab for anything that took his fancy, whether it be a swag of cash money – or even a close friend's woman.

He turned back to the yard to sight the Traffords returning from the mine. Tom Trafford might be large, strong and wealthy but had a lot to learn about women, he mused. Husbands, from his own observations, tended to take their women for granted after a time. That was almost inviting somebody who genuinely knew how to treat a female to slip under their guard. Someone just like him, maybe. . . .

He joined the workers and they entered the house together. Soon the sounds of pleasant conversation and easy laughter were to be heard again on Maverick Ranch.

McCoy sighted the buzzard first, a solitary, yellow-beaked eminence perched on the upper branch of a dead mesquite tree some distance to the north.

Gaunt and played out at the end of long days of fruitless searching in the badlands, the bounty hunter didn't pay the ugly bird any particular attention until he saw it launch its ungainly body from the tree and drop down into a Lizard Desert arroyo.

'Could be somethin' dead up there, Mallone,' he muttered. 'Wanna go take a look?'

Grizzled and sun-blackened with dust in his beard stubble, Mallone screwed up his eyes against the glare coming off the shimmering wastes. At last he shrugged. 'Why not?' and they turned their cayuses and rode north.

The buzzard gave a raucous shriek at their

approach and immediately flew back to its dead tree, landing clumsily. There was just the one bird and as they reined in on the rim of the arroyo the bounty hunters saw why there weren't more.

The ghastly white bones of two dead men and three horses scattered across the floor of the arroyo had been picked clean.

Suddenly McCoy and Mallone weren't weary any longer. They traded silent glances and started on down.

A quick inspection of the dead established they had all been shot. The surrounding rocks were liberally bullet-scarred and one of the skeletons had a slug embedded in the skull. Scouting further along the arroyo they found the remains of a third man.

Returning to the ambush site they rifled the saddle-bags strapped to the dead animals to find whiskey, canned meat, several boxes of shells and two black bandannas.

The outlaws who'd robbed the Mercurio bank had worn black masks.

McCoy stared at his partner. 'You figure Clanton caught up with them?

Mallone shook his head. 'He'd have toted them back to Mercurio if he had. Or planted them, at least.'

'Unless he got beefed too?' Mallone rose and slouched across to the twin grey boulders where the bullet scars showed most prominently.

'Looks to me like one man waited up here and cut the other two down,' he opined. 'Then I guess the two left fought it out between themselves over who got the dinero.'

McCoy licked his lips. 'That money might still be some place close about, Mallone.'

'Mebbe so. Let's go take a look.'

They searched throughout what was left of the afternoon until the sun went down. They found no sign of the money, nothing of the fourth outlaw nor anything that might disprove Mallone's theory that what they had stumbled upon was simply the grisly outcome of a falling-out amongst thieves and and a battle to the death between the Mercurio oulaws.

They were soon forced to rug up against the chill desert wind before starting off just as the first stars winked out. There was plenty to occupy the minds of each, along with a decision to reach. Mallone was first to break the silence.

'We'll make for the nearest town and find out if the law caught up with them or not,' he decided. 'If there's no news then I reckon we can claim that they shot it out between themselves and that the last geezer still standin' got off with the money.'

'Makes sense I guess. But then what? Wouldn't he be long gone, Mallone?'

'Mebbe, mebbe not,' Mallone shivered as a chilly gust struck from behind. 'Judas Priest, this here wind is too lazy to go round a man so it just cuts right through. Pass that whiskey.'

McCoy handed the bottle across as the moon peered over the horizon to bathe the desert with its cold metallic light. Far off across the sandy reaches, a wolf howled mournfully. It was a ghostly sound and lonesome. The riders heeled the horses into a lope and the wind got busy brushing sand into the hoofprints they left behind.

The bellowing of the cattle came down from the trees flanking the uneven slopes around Five Mile Sink as weary Maverick hands pushed the bunch on towards the corrals. The cattle were thirsty from the drive and had already caught the scent of water at the sink. A flock of jaybirds rose out of the trees, screeching in annoyance as the cattle emerged from the timber.

It was five hundred yards from the timber to the water and the animals covered it at a ragged trot. There were around fifty in the bunch, a small herd which normally grazed at South Mesa but which had been brought back to the Five Mile to fatten up for marketing. The riders spurred on ahead to slow the animals' progress to ensure they didn't trample one another in their eagerness to get in and drink.

Luke Trafford swabbed sweat from his face as he pulled his horse to a halt at the rim of the sink.

Mustering the half-wild stock had been hard work made more difficult by the fact that he didn't really have enough men to do the job properly. The Maverick was due to ship its gold south to the bank in Phoenix shortly and his brothers were employing most of the men in the mine in an effort to catch up on the production schedule.

Clay Grady and Zac Stannard rode by on the far side of the water. 'We're cutting back for that baldy-faced steer we lost in the brush, Luke!' Grady called.

'Don't overdo it!' Luke shouted back with a grin. A horseman approached through the dust billows and Luke identified the slender figure of Lee. The boy had worked as hard as any man yet was still smiling as he reined in at his side. Lee was like himself. He hated the mine but loved working with cattle.

'Kentucky wants to know if he should brew some coffee, Luke.'

'Sure, why not? Tom'll only saddle us with more work if we get back too early.'

With a yip, Lee spurred off through the dust again, leaving Luke to supervise the cattle until he was called across to the line-rider's shack for the coffee.

It was the mildest day of the summer and Trafford, Lee, Kentucky and Billy Jills all hunkered down comfortably in the sun watching the now-satisfied cattle begin to spread out over the graze.

The talk was mostly of cattle and branding, beef prices and the shipment to Phoenix. They smoked cigarettes lazily and presently saw Zac Stannard appear over the grassy swells below the trees with a chastened baldy-faced steer trotting ahead of him.

'Where's Clay?' Lee asked as Stannard rode up.

'Took sick,' the cowboy replied, swinging down. He nodded at Luke. 'Got the cramps when we were up along Blue Ridge, Luke. So he said, leastwise. If you ask me, he's just doin' too much too quick.'

'Damn!' Luke said, rising. 'I warned him to ease off. I'd best go catch him up.'

'Better hold up a minute there, Luke,' Stannard said. 'There's a rider comin' in from the west. We sighted him just about the time Clay took sick. Looked to me like he was wearin' a star, this geezer. I was fixin' to wait and see what he wanted, only that steer was actin' so cussed I had to bring him in instead. Reckon that feller would see all the dust down here clear enough anyways.'

'Looks like it, Zac,' Kentucky said, pointing. 'Yonder he comes now.'

The man with the badge rode in slowly around the sink. He was middle-aged and of spare build with the sort of face that looked like it belonged behind a star. He dismounted stiffly by the shack and let the reins trail as he came forward.

'Afternoon, gents,' he greeted. 'Sheriff Clanton from Utah. This is the Maverick Ranch, isn't it?'

'Sure is, Sheriff,' Luke said, extending his hand. 'Luke Trafford.'

Canton shook hands. 'This your spread, Luke?'

'My brother's and mine. What can we do for you, Sheriff?'

Clanton smiled. 'Well, you might pour me a mug of that coffee if you have it to spare. Smells good.'

'Forgettin' our manners,' Kentucky grinned, filling a pannikin. 'Here you go, Sheriff.'

'Much obliged.' Clanton took a swig and looked around. 'Nice outfit you have here, Luke. Biggest spread in the region, so I'm told.'

'That's so,' Luke replied.

'And good coffee,' Clanton said. 'Tell me, Luke, have you seen any strangers about over the last few weeks? I've been hunting a dog pack of outlaws who robbed the bank in Mercurio, Utah Territory. I lost the sign in the Lizard Desert more than a week back now. I searched every mile down to the Capitans without success, now I'm working my way up through the cattle country.'

'Outlaws?' Lee said, wide-eyed. 'Hell, we haven't seen an outlaw in these parts for years, Sheriff.'

'No strangers around at all?' Clanton pressed. 'You haven't hired any new men recent?'

'Nary a one, Sheriff,' Luke supplied. 'Haven't sighted any strangers neither. Sorry.'

'That's all right, Luke.' The sheriff managed a weary smile. 'I'm probably licked but I just don't know it, if the truth be told. Reckon I'd just better admit that they've licked me.'

'When did you lose them fellers, Sheriff?' Kentucky wanted to know. 'About a week back, did you say?'

'That's right,' Clanton replied.

Kentucky glanced at Luke. 'That would be about the time Grady got jumped by them camp robbers over at Rogue River, Luke. Wonder if that could've been them outlaws?'

Clanton glanced sharply at Kentucky. 'Camp robbers you say? How many?'

'I don't reckon Clay rightly knew how many there were, Sheriff,' Luke declared. 'Clay Grady's an old war buddy of mine who came over recent to visit from Arizona. These hardcases shot him up some but he came out of it all right. He's been convalescing at our spread with us ever since.'

'Why, I'd like to speak to this friend of yours, Luke. This just might be the lead I'm hunting for.'

'Sure. Grady would be happy to tell you anything he can, Sheriff. If he's up to talking, that is. He was working out here with us today but took poorly just a while ago and had to ride back.'

'I see.'

'Well, let's go take a look,' Luke offered. 'We're all through here anyway. And you're welcome to take supper with us if you're of a mind, Sheriff. My sister-in-law is about the finest cook in the territory.'

'That sounds like the best offer I've had since I left home,' Clanton grinned. 'Thank you kindly.'

Collecting their gear the party mounted up and started off. They had traveled some distance before Luke realized a rider was lagging behind.

'Get a shake on, Kentucky!' he called back. 'Otherwise folks will start getting the notion you're too old to keep pace any more.'

Kentucky heeled his horse up to join them. But Luke noted the old man didn't speak all the long way back to headquarters. Instead, Kentucky rode like a man with weighty matters on his mind.

*

Clay Grady said he didn't feel up to talking with the sheriff of Mercurio either that night or the following morning after Clanton had stayed over specifically in the hope of discussing the events of Rogue River with him.

Virna was puzzled by his relapse and all she could think of was that he might be bleeding internally. She wanted to send for the medic in Apollo City but Grady insisted that all he required was rest and all the peace and quiet he could get.

The sheriff was plainly disappointed, even after Grady had afforded a full, detailed account of the Rogue River incident to Luke, who in turn passed it on to the peace officer.

The sheriff showed he was even willing to delay another day or two in the hope that Grady might still recover sufficiently to grant him an audience, but Luke firmly dissuaded him from doing so.

His only concern was for his old friend, he pointed out. And as Grady was adamant he wasn't up to any kind of interrogation, Luke saw his duty of responsibility as quite plain. No interview.

His stand was suppported strongly by Tom and, very firmly, by Virna. So, rather than run the risk of offending members of one of the most highly respected families in the county by insisting on consulting their friend, Ben Clanton decided to be content with what little he'd heard second-hand, and eventually took his leave.

That night, Grady's sudden bout of weakness left him as quickly as it had come. Virna was delighted when he appeared for supper and, having taken no food in twenty-four hours, promptly disposed of a hearty three-course meal, plus the trimmings.

Although quiet and withdrawn while they ate, Grady picked up over brandy and cigars in the big front room afterwards, taking a keen interest now in the visit of Sheriff Clanton.

'You know, Luke,' he remarked, 'I feel now that maybe I should have made the effort and seen that peace officer. Yeah, I know I told you everything I recalled about the camp robbers. But maybe if I'd spoken to Clanton direct he might have picked upon on something of value to him. Wonder if I could catch him up in Apollo City?'

'Forget it!' Luke was emphatic. 'What happened yesterday showed you're not halfway near as fit as you think you are. You won't be going any place until I give the say-so, Lieutenant.'

Clay Grady lifted his hands in resignation then let them drop back to the armrests of his leather chair. He didn't mention Sheriff Clanton again and, watching from a corner where he sat nursing his glass, Kentucky would have been surprised if he had.

The old man didn't touch his drink. Suspicion was strong in him now, so strong that it almost turned his stomach to think of the effect it would have on the Traffords if what he half-suspected should turn out to be rooted in truth.

Kentucky had never been in such a quandary. From the outset something about Clayton Grady had struck him as not quite right. It was nothing more than instinct at first but had been strengthened over time by a sequence of little things, like that damaged saddle the man had carried in, his evasiveness about his years since the war culminating in what had happened yesterday and today.

The old-timer had questioned Zac Stannard closely and was certain now that Grady had seen Sheriff Clanton out by the Five Mile Sink and had immediately 'taken ill'. This, along with Grady's refusal to see the lawman, followed by his remarkable recovery here tonight, convinced Kentucky that for some reason Grady had been afraid to meet that peace officer face to face.

And this posed the big question. Why?

Kentucky didn't like any of the answers that sprang to mind. And the one he liked least of all was that which suggested that Luke's old army friend could be one of the bank robbers from Utah.

Kentucky shook his grey head like an old horse being tormented by flies. Back in his secret past which he shared with no man, he'd once had a family, a family which had been ground to dust beneath a wartime juggernaut known as Sherman's Legions.

A man adrift, Kentucky had eventually come to the Maverick Ranch in Arizona and found himself another family. He cared for them as strongly as he had for his own. He would protect them with his life. All those fierce sentiments burned in him now . . . but how did one protect a man from his friend?

He glanced across at Clay Grady who smiled and nodded at something Virna was saying.

I must be wrong, Kentucky told himself grimly. Yet some small, stubborn part of him wouldn't let him believe that.

SEVEN

MAVERICK MOON

The deep hush of midnight hung over Maverick Ranch.

The breeze that blew in every night from the desert rippled the leaves of the oaks and cottonwoods and raised a faint wraith of fog about the lamplit mine mouth where two sentries paced out their watch before the sturdy doors of the gold room.

Standing by the window of his darkened room, Clay Grady looked out at the night, hands hooked in shell belt, one shoulder leaning against the frame and a small cigar dangling from his lips.

He was smiling as he reflected how life always seemed better with a dash of danger in it. The arrival and departure of the Mercurio lawman had honed his senses sharp. And he took pride in the way he had so adroitly handled the visit of the peace officer without raising any suspicions in anybody, including the badgeman.

But he wasn't about to count himself safely out of the woods just yet. A lawman had come sniffing about the Maverick, and there was no guarantee he might not be back.

His fingers brushed gunbutt and the smile came again. He knew he couldn't pull his relapse trick a second time . . . so who could tell? If put to it, he might yet have to rely upon the good old reliable sixer riding his right hip should that badgetoter come up with any new suspicions about him. He would never allow a lawman to take him either alive or dead.

But the .45 would be the last resort, he promised himself. His best bet was simply to stick close to the Maverick, play up his friendship with the clan and then simply bide his time . . . always aware now that if there was one badgetoter sniffing about there could easily be more.

He stiffened as a figure emerged from the bunkhouse and stood in the shadows looking up toward the house.

He realized it was that crafty-eyed old waddy,

Kentucky. The lean figure stood there on the stoop for maybe a minute, then stepped out into the flooding moonlight and strolled off toward the stables where a dim light showed. The doors opened and he disappeared inside.

Grady stroked his smooth-shaven jaw, the crease between his brows cutting deeper now. The old man's appearance puzzled him. For Kentucky had been acting strangely toward him almost from the outset. He couldn't figure why. But something was plainly making the old feller restless tonight, and suddenly it occurred to him that maybe he should try to find out just what that might be.

He acted on the impulse, stepping down and starting across the yard. The wind-borne scents of sage, wild flowers and grass feathered his senses. Everything tasted sweet to him tonight and he was feeling free, powerful and ready for anything.

He eased the stable door open silently and stepped inside. Kentucky's flung shadow showed hugely upon a wall. The old man sat upon a three-legged stool with the lantern planted on the floor before him. He had his back to the door and a saddle rested upon his knee.

Grady's saddle.

For the second time in minutes Grady's right hand flew to gunbutt. He stood motionless for some time with a cold glitter in his eyes. Then with a small shake of his head he took his hand off the gun handle, fixed a big smile to his face and stepped inside into the light.

'Killed a Chinaman, Kentucky?'

The old man started at his sudden voice, yet not as sharply as Grady might have expected. Good nerves, he noted. Plainly not a man to be sold short.

'Why, howdy Grady,' Kentucky replied, seemingly unfazed. 'What was that about a Chinaman?'

Grady leaned one hand upon a scarred workbench.

'They say if a man kills a Chinaman he can't ever get to sleep nights,' he smiled.

'Well, I don't know beans about Chinamen, but I sure sleep good.' Kentucky tapped the saddle on his lap. 'Always find there's nothing like takin' on a chore or two at times like that. So I figured I'd do some fixin' on your saddle.'

'Without tools? Not a bad trick that.'

'I was checkin' to see what had to be done first.'

'Funny thing, but I'm pondering that same thing right now.' A long pause. 'What needs to be done. . . .'

'I don't follow.'

'I mean . . . what am I going to do about you, old-timer?' Grady broke off to let him worry about that for a moment, then added smilingly, 'I'm talking about the fact of you not liking me, of course. Now, what should a man do about that?'

'You got me wrong.'

'Have I? But that saddle of mine bothers you, doesn't it Kentucky? Any good reason why it should?'

'Just curious, I guess.'

'You heard that curiosity killed the cat, I reckon?'

Kentucky's eyes turned flinty as he rose. 'You tryin' to scare me, boy? I never did scare a lick.'

Grady studied that seamed old face and felt an odd prickling of his skin. It came as a sudden shock to realize that this ancient retainer of the Traffords was, beneath his laconic exterior, a dangerous man. Grady was never wrong about things like that.

He licked his lips and said, 'What's your real story, old-timer? Just who are you anyway?'

'Just an old cracker who's bent on seein' that folks he cares about don't come to grief, I guess.'

'And you think I might hurt them? What do you figure I might do? Steal their gold? Run off with the silver service, mebbe?'

'You tell me.'

Grady suddenly smiled. 'Listen to us sniping at one another, old man. You think heaps of the Traffords, and so do I. We're the same, and both on the same side. So why are we sniping this way?'

'I ain't sure. But if I could figure what happened to this here saddle and how come you hung onto it even when you were half dead. That always kinda puzzled me some. . . .'

'Easy to explain. This saddle is an old friend. I used it right through the war. There was no way I was going to leave it after Appomattox, and when it got too heavy to tote about I ripped the stuffing out to make it lighter to carry. *Sabe*?'

He gave Kentucky time to consider what he'd said, then continued.

'Look, I'll level with you, old man. Yes, I have raised some hell since the war, and I'm not exactly the upright gent Luke might reckon. But one thing I am is his good friend. I want you to believe that.'

Kentucky massaged his face, finally nodded. He rose to replace the damaged saddle on a tree. 'Guess I could be wrong about you, Grady. And I can't deny you've given this place some kind of boost it needed. . . .'

'Then we're friends and understand one another?'

'Reckon so.'

'Then why don't we shake?'

They shook. Yet Grady could not be certain he'd won the old man over. He should stay wary of this one, he told himself as they went out into the night together.

'Goodnight, old-timer.'

' 'Night, Grady,' Kentucky murmured, and headed upslope for the bunkhouse.

Torching up another cigar, Grady set off on a rambling circuit around the night guards. Later, he felt curiosity stir when he stopped to look across at the heavy, iron-hinged door of the gold room, reacting as he always had done at even the faintest whiff of big money, any place, any time.

He shook his head firmly and continued on. No. He had told the old man the truth when he'd claimed to have no interest in the gold workings. He wasn't greedy – he had all he needed.

Then he laughed softly, couldn't help it. For the truth was that greed was his god. Always was and always would be.

'You're not hungry, Luke?'

'Sorry, Virna. Maybe I didn't sleep so good, I guess.'

She smiled. 'Not a guilty conscience, I hope?'

'Wish it was that simple.'

It was quiet for a moment around the breakfast table. Then Tom Trafford said, 'Something's bothering you, Luke, I could always tell. Why don't you share it?'

'Just not hungry I guess,' Luke replied, rising and making for the breakfast-room door. He paused and grinned. 'I'll go roll a quirley. Never went to tobacco for a lift when it didn't work.'

Out on the porch with the cigarette clamped between his teeth, he rested hands on hips and frowned at the new day. For he knew exactly what was bothering him, yet wasn't certain he understood why this should be so.

Grady.

It was as simple as that – or as complicated. Right from the day and the hour his wartime partner had shown up out of no place there had been this feeling of unease clouding the pleasure he should have felt at their reunion.

How come?

He'd figured the answer to that as well. Grady had changed. Either that or he had changed himself. Whatever the case, he knew Grady was different from what he remembered, and the change was not an improvement. At times he felt almost alienated from the man, somehow suspicious. Could that indicate he'd simply become staid and stodgy without a raging war to fire him up while Clay Grady had remained headstrong, reckless and somehow unknowable?

He shook his head. Someone was calling to him from the horse yards. He thrust Grady from his thoughts as he went down the steps, yet that strange uneasiness remained.

He got rid of it once he was working, yet knew it would come back.

Through the vee formed by his crossed black boots resting upon the saloon porch railing, Mallone watched Apollo City in the morning.

Shoppers and tradesmen moved to and fro along the plankwalks and horse and wagon traffic was heavy down Main Street. His cigar had gone out but he'd not bothered to light it up again. McCoy sat by his side whittling a piece of deal board with a bowie knife. They were serving liquor inside but the bounty hunters were going without whiskey at the moment, mainly to help their funds spin out.

Apollo City had come up empty for them. No word of any dead men in the desert, nothing to suggest their man had ventured anywhere near this crummy town. Once again it seemed the trail had gone cold.

'I'm starvin', Mallone.'

'You could live off your tat for a year.'

'Dry, too.'

'There's a trough yonder.'

'You ain't like me, Mallone. You can get by just by feedin' on your cussedness. You live for money but I'm a eatin' and drinkin' man.'

'Give me a light and button up, will you.'

With a gusty sigh McCoy snapped a vesta into life on a grimy thumbnail. He held the flame to the battered stogie jutting from his partner's pearly white teeth, but Mallone appeared too lethargic even to do the drawback. Then he realized the other was staring fixedly at something across the street. Following the line of his gaze, McCoy instantly stiffened.

Moving along the opposite plankwalk with tireless step, was Sheriff Ben Clanton of Mercurio.

Both bounty hunters leaned forward intently to watch the lawman pause to speak with a passer-by before starting across the street.

'Now what the hell is that one doin' hereabouts, Mallone?'

'Same thing we are, I'm guessin'. By Judas, this could be a sign we're hotter than we realized, McCoy!' Mallone rose sharply. 'C'mon, better make ourselves scarce before that John Law sights us.'

'Too late,' McCoy said. 'He's comin' straight for us.'

Mallone mashed his stogie with his teeth, spat it out, then flopped back into his chair. He quickly raised his boots up on the railing then tipped his sorry hat over his eyes to appear relaxed. But McCoy looked nervous and was sweating a little as Clanton mounted the steps. Lawmen always had that effect upon McCoy, even though, technically at least, they were both on the same side of the fence in the eyes of the law.

They knew Clanton as a direct man. He was direct now.

'What are you two doing here?'

McCoy glanced at Mallone. Mallone was studying his fingernails with great concentration. So McCoy cleared his throat and fixed a smile on his homely mug.

'Howdy there, Sheriff. Right pretty weather we're havin'.'

'I asked you a question, wiseacre.' Clanton elbowed Mallone's boots off the railing. 'I'm asking *you*!'

Slowly, Mallone fingered his battered hat back. He didn't like lawmen either but they did not make him nervous. He took his slow time answering.

'Earnin' a livin', Clanton. What's your excuse?'

'How long have you been in town?'

'Long enough.'

'Look, mister—'

'No, you look, Clanton. We're law-abidin' citizens

and we got as much right to put our feet up wherever we please without any interference from geezers who figure a tin star makes 'em special.'

Mallone put his boots up again. 'You're blockin' the view.'

Clanton nodded, tight-lipped.

'You're right of course, Mallone. On paper, at least, you are both respectable citizens. Which is something of a reflection on the laws of this country. You're free to come and go as you please and will continue to be until I or someone like me can prove otherwise. Then you'll both end up where you belong. Doing twenty years apiece.'

Mallone's smirk was offensive.

'You're crochety, Clanton. How come? Peeved on account them big bad bank robbers gave you the slip?'

Clanton swore viciously and made off without answering to head directly for the sheriff's office. Two sets of unblinking eyes followed his every step.

Mallone leaned forward. 'He's turnin' in at the jailhouse, McCoy. That long-snout is onto somethin' sure enough, and sooner or later you and me is gonna find out what it is.' He rose. 'C'mon, pard, I'll buy you a shot.'

McCoy came out of his chair fast. He'd seldom felt more like a stiff brandy. Or maybe two.

Sheriff Bob Mosby knew nothing of any robbery attempt at Rogue River. Nor was he even aware that a friend of Luke Trafford's was staying out at Maverick Ranch. The local lawman also regretted to inform Sheriff Clanton that he had never heard the name Clayton Grady before, and wanted to know why Sheriff Clanton seemed suspicious of the man.

Yet Clanton hadn't actually been suspicious – until now. He was merely following routine procedures in checking and verifying everything he'd learned during the course of his investigations. Now he puzzled why nobody outside the Maverick Ranch seemed concerned about the camp-robbers' attack at Rogue River.

That was not all Ben Clanton had on his mind as he sat discussing the Mercurio robbery and Maverick Ranch with the sheriff of Apollo City. In addition there was also the unsettling presence here of Mallone and McCoy to be considered.

Clanton knew the bounty hunters as well as he needed to. McCoy was a blunt axe but Mallone was a rapier. Mallone's record in bringing badmen to book was proof enough the man was a highly skilled hunter of men.

Clanton no longer believed it was mere chance

that had brought the pair to Apollo City. Their tenacity on a job paralleled his own.

It would take a lot of convincing to persuade him that the bounty hunters had not followed some lead to Apollo City. And this, in turn, brought him back to the mystery surrounding Clayton Grady's presence in the region.

It couldn't do any harm, so he told himself as he quit the office a short time later, to go check that man out.

That was what led him firstly to the Apollo City telegraph office situated on the corner of Main and Trail. From there he sent off wires to both his headquarters in Mercurio, to the marshals in Salt Lake City and also the offices of Utah Territory Law Agencies at Medicine Bow.

Each message was brief and identical:

PLEASE FURNISH ANY INFORMATION
AVAILABLE ON CLAYTON GRADY,
UNION ARMY VETERAN. NO OTHER
FACTS KNOWN.

That done, Ben Clanton checked into the City Hotel and settled down to wait.

Virna and Tom Trafford were arguing in the ranch

house kitchen next morning when Clayton Grady walked in. The discussion concerned their proposed trip to town later in the day. It was Saturday and Virna wanted the family to visit Apollo City for some badly needed rest and relaxation.

Tom, despite the fact that he and his men had been working twelve hour shifts daily in preparation for the shipment of gold to Phoenix, wanted to work until sundown then drive into Apollo City at night.

Unknown to Grady, both Luke and Lee were sitting on the back porch waiting to find out who would win the debate.

The discussion broke off when the couple finally grew aware of Grady's presence as he moved to lean lazily in the doorway. He smiled when the couple turned his way.

'Hope I'm not intruding, folks.'

'Of course not, Clay,' Virna said, looking flushed and very pretty. 'We were just finalising plans to visit town . . . this *afternoon*!'

'Tonight,' Tom said stubbornly. 'You care to join us, Clay?'

'Reckon I might pass, Tom. That turn I took scared me. But I reckon you two will enjoy it. And why not go early? Nothing like bright lights and fresh faces to bring back the bloom to a lady's cheeks, they say.'

'See, Tom Trafford,' Virna said spiritedly. 'Clay understands.'

Big Tom's heavy jaw shot out. 'I don't recall asking for any outside advice.'

'My mistake, Tom,' Grady said easily. 'I'll leave you folks to it, like I should.'

'No, don't go, Clay,' Virna said, noisily clattering her pots and pans now. 'It's so pleasant to have the company of a real gentleman, I can assure you.'

Something that could have been jealousy flickered in Tom Trafford's eyes as he glanced from his wife to the handsome Grady. Then he abruptly turned and headed for the door.

'All right!' he barked over his shoulder. 'We'll go at three!'

'How gracious of you, darling,' Virna called after him, but Tom gave no sign he'd heard. Grady expected to hear the front door slam but it didn't.

'He's a good man, Virna,' Grady said easily. 'Just doesn't stop to think sometimes, I guess.'

Virna had her back to him at the washbasin as she replied, 'He never thinks these days. It's all the fault of that stupid mine. It's all he ever seems to think of.'

'A man's a fool to neglect a woman like you, Virna. I'm sure I wouldn't.'

She didn't reply. She appeared too angry. Grady watched the way her slender body moved beneath the dress and how the dark hair clung softly to the nape of her neck.

He made no sound as he crossed the room. Her first awareness of his nearness was when his arms slid around her waist.

'Clay!' she gasped, turning sharply, and that was the moment Luke and Lee came through the door leading onto the porch.

For a moment nobody moved. Then with a furious gesture, Virna thrust Grady away and rushed from the room.

Lee's face flushed. 'What the hell! What do you think you're doin', Clay?'

Grady was rueful as he raised both hands then let them drop.

'Your sister was upset from wrangling with Tom, Lee. I was just trying to comfort her, is all.'

'It looked more than that to me,' Lee said heatedly. 'I don't like what I saw, Clay.'

'It's all right, Lee,' Luke said quietly. 'It was nothing, I'm sure. You go on along to the corrals. I want a word with Clay.'

With a final angry glance at Grady, Lee quit the room. An uncomfortable silence fell as Grady and Luke stood facing. It was finally broken by Grady.

'You believe me, don't you, Luke?'

'I said I did, didn't I?' But then, 'You always were a dab hand with the ladies, as I recall, Clay.'

'Damnit all, man, do you think I'd repay your hospitality by making a fool play for Virna?'

'A real dab hand,' Luke said, as though the other had not spoken.

'Well, you sure disappoint me, Luke. I figured we knew one another better than that. I reckon I'll leave today.'

Luke turned to study him again. 'No call to do that, Clay. I want you to stay on . . . at least until you're fully recovered, longer if you want. But . . . well, I guess you know what I mean to say next?'

'Don't let it happen again?' Grady anticipated. 'No chance.' He clapped a hand to Luke's shoulder. 'I realize now it was a dumb thing to do, even if I meant no harm. No hard feelings?'

'It's forgotten, Clay. Now, I'd best go see Lee. I don't want him saying anything to Tom.'

'You reckon he might?'

'He's riled. He just could do.'

'Well, if that's the case it's up to me to convince him that there was nothing to it. I made the mistake, so I'll correct it.'

'Maybe that would be best.'

'Good as done,' Grady assured, going out. 'See

you at lunch – pard.'

Heading for the corrals, Clay Grady was feeling proud of the adroit way he'd handled Luke. Yet it proved more difficult with Lee. Lee was not a friend of long standing who might be ready to give him the benefit of the doubt, as was Luke. Grady was aware the boy had developed an admiration for him since his coming to the spread, but what he'd seen in the house today had plainly shaken his belief in his new hero.

The boy listened sullenly while Grady did some slick talking over several minutes. Grady believed he'd made headway, but still could not be sure Lee might not go to Big Tom with his version of events.

He couldn't risk that happening.

Tom Trafford was no man to tangle with and just might hand him his marching orders. Grady wanted to avoid that – for strong reasons of his own.

'Look, Lee, you don't know me like your Uncle Luke does. He accepted my explanation, so isn't that enough to convince you there was nothing to it?'

'I saw what I saw!'

'Well, if that's how you feel, boy,' he said dramatically, not meaning a word of it, 'I'll just go pack.'

Lee weakened at that. 'Hell, I didn't say I wanted

you to go, Clay.'

'I'd have no choice if you spoke to Tom.'

'All right, let's forget it. That's it, done and dusted. OK?'

'Spoken like a man. OK, what I'm about to do has nothing to do with what we just talked about. It's just that I can recall what it was like to be your age. So, here's something to help make sure you have yourself a fine time of it in Apollo City.'

He pressed something into Lee's hand. When he saw it was a one-hundred dollar bill, the boy couldn't believe it.

'Glory be, Clay, I can't take that. I've never had that much money in my—'

'Well, you have now . . . and I won't even say spend it wisely. So . . . shake?'

Lee grabbed his hand. 'Thanks again, Clay.'

'Any time, boy, any time. . . .'

Grady inhaled deeply as he stode off across the yard. That had been a close one. He'd had to get the boy onside, now it was Virna's turn. For reasons known only to himself he needed a safe haven here at least until he was fully recovered. Then he could deal with anything that might come his way – just like always.

His confidence was borne out when he entered the house and sought out Virna. She accepted his explanation and insisted no more be said. She was very cool, but he'd expected that. She would warm to him again in time. They always did ... and Clayton Grady always came out a winner.

No matter what.

EIGHT

CHEAP WHISKEY, ROUGH COMPANY

The grizzled telegrapher glanced up from his key board as the door opened to admit the lean figure of the sheriff of Mercurio.

'Afternoon, Sheriff Clanton. Something I can do for you?'

'Any messages for me, Mr Smythe?'

'Only that one we delivered to you this mornin', Sheriff. The one from Medicine Bow to tell you they didn't seem to know anythin' about that there Grady feller.'

'I see. . . .' Clanton leaned an elbow on the counter. 'Mr Smythe, I'd appreciate it if you didn't disclose any details outside this office relating to any messages I might send or receive just now. You understand?'

'Of course, Sheriff. Heck, I'm not one of your gabby telegraphers that gets to spreadin' folks business all over the place.'

'I'm sure you're not.'

'But you're wastin' your time and money, you realize?'

'I am? How so?'

'If this feller you're interested in is a pard of Luke Trafford's, then you can bet your last dollar he's straight as a gun barrel. There ain't a straighter man in the county than Luke.'

'I'm sure you're right about that.' Clanton straightened. 'Well, I know I can count on you to get any message that might come through to me poste haste, and I thank you for that, Mr Smythe.'

'Just doin' my job. Oh, by the way, Sheriff, you realize the office will be closed tomorrow.' The man smiled. 'A man must have his day of rest on the Sabbath, right?'

'In most professsions that rule applies, leastwise. Mr Smythe. Not mine. Well, good day to you.'

'So long, Sheriff.'

Two hours later and Main Street was bustling with Saturday afternoon traffic. The cowhands were coming in from the outlying spreads with money in their Levis and the saloons were already doing good business.

Clanton leaned a shoulder against an upright and serviced his teeth with a small, silver toothpick. He had just come from lunch with Sheriff Bob Mosby at Greasy Kate's. Mosby was investigating the alleged attack at Rogue River but had uncovered nothing. Mosby's attitude suggested he would have been surprised had anything come to light. Whoever had been involved had operated like genuine professionals, which could only concern any sober and hard-working lawman.

Fortunately, this town was maintaining its reputation as peaceful and hard-working, a place where the even ebb and flow of country life was largely undisturbed by violence or major crime.

The lawman nodded to himself, a man at one with this solid town and maybe a little complacent as he gazed around. No hint of outlaws and no shady tupes spending up big with no explanation of how they'd come by their big dinero. Nothing but honest faces and easy smiles all around.

With two notable exceptions.

Clanton drew the pick from his teeth when he sighted Mallone and McCoy swing into Main from Gulliver Street and travel along the plankwalk like they owned it while making for the Sundown Saloon.

Clanton's day was now ruined. Everywhere he turned these days it seemed that sooner or later this pair would show: loafing on porch benches, slouching about the streets with no visible means of support, talking with the locals and, of course, hooting and whistling whenever a pair of pretty ankles twinkled past.

By this, the lawman figured the bounty hunters must be on the scent of something here. He'd been told the pair were constantly asking questions about strangers.

What did they know?

Shaking his head, Clanton started off along the street in the opposite direction. He realized he was getting irritable these days and his horse was getting fat. He would do something for them both this very afternoon by taking a ride. But like always, he would be back by sundown.

Luke Trafford could hear Lee and Tom arguing up ahead as he rode the trail to town at Kentucky's side. This didn't surprise him any for Tom had been in testy temper ever since his wrangle with Virna that morning.

Luke was an easygoing man but was growing

weary of all the friction these days. He was further troubled by feelings of disloyalty whenever he found himself placing most of the blame for trouble at his brother's feet.

But Tom had changed and he had to face that fact. More and more Tom was acting like somebody who put business first and all else second. He was getting to be a pain in the rear end and Luke wondered how long it might be before he felt forced to take big brother out behind the barn and thump some horse sense into him.

He grinned at the very thought. That would be the day! Tom had always been able to whip him and probably still could.

'Well, I'm right pleased somebody's happy at least,' Kentucky observed wryly, catching his grin.

'You're happy too, old-timer,' Luke replied. 'You always are when you're on your way to wrap yourself around a skinful of booze.'

'I can drink you under the table on the best day you ever had, boy.'

'I'll admit that at drinking you're a champion, Kentucky. But at working? Well now, that is surely a skunk of a different stripe.'

Kentucky chuckled. He was enjoying just riding in the sun with Luke and lightening the journey to town sharing jokes and insults. Yet the scene up front was bothering him just a little.

'Wonder what Tom's griping about now?' he asked after a silence.

Luke looked ahead to where Lee rode alongside the ranch surrey. 'Lee just forgot to do somethin' afore we left. Nothin' worth frettin' about. But you know Tom.'

'Thought I did.'

Luke sobered. 'He's going too hard, Kentucky. After we ship the gold to Phoenix on Tuesday, I aim to tell him to take a break away. Him and Virna. They need it.'

'Won't get any argument from me on that one. Hell! The kid's just taken off!'

Lee was indeed spurring off in a temper along the trail. Virna called after him but the boy didn't turn. When Luke and Kentucky rode up abreast of the surrey, the couple were arguing. Again.

'What happened?' Luke queried.

'Ask your brother, Luke,' Virna said. 'It was all his fault.'

'Fool kid just flew off the handle when I told him I didn't want him drinkin' too much in town, is all,' Tom growled. 'You'd better get after him, Luke. He listens to you but not to me.'

'That's because you bark at him,' Virna chided. 'Please, Luke, go fetch him back.'

'No, we'll let him go, Virna,' Luke decided. 'Could be it will do him good to get away from all of us on his lonesome for a spell. He'll be all right.'

'He's a hot-headed young fool,' Tom countered.

'He's a fine boy,' Virna disagreed, as Luke and Kennedy allowed their horses to drop back.

'Nothin' like a nice happy little trip to town, young Luke.'

'Nothing like it, old-timer. And you know, I just might have to take you up on that challenge of yours.'

'What challenge is that?'

'To drink me under the table.'

Kentucky laughed. 'You're on.'

The percentage girl who sidled up to the young man at the bar of the Jimcrack Saloon wore a brief, spangled red dress with silk stockings and carried a feather boa. Her smile was white and welcoming.

'Why, Lee Clarke. What brings you down to the seamy side of town? Does your sister know you're slummin', honey?'

Lee smiled at her. He'd had two quick shots and was feeling fine again.

'Howdy, Miss Kitty. Buy you a drink?'

'That's what I'm here for, sweetie,' she said, climbing onto a bar stool with a swish of silk. She stirred the air before her face with a mother-of-pearl fan. 'But I'm still curious. You Trafford folks never come down to see little old Kitty at the Jimcrack.'

'Well, maybe that's why I came today,' he said, spinning a coin onto the bar top. 'Another shot, Jake, and whatever Miss Kitty drinks.'

'You sound like a man plannin' a real big night of it, honey,' the girl remarked.

'That's me. One big night comin' up.'

'Your folks come in with you today?' she asked as the drinks were served.

'Sure did. Cheers, Miss Kitty.'

'Lookin' at you.' Kitty lowered her glass. 'That feller you got stayin' with you out there come in with you? That Grady feller?'

'How'd you know about him?'

'Why, that li'l old sheriff from Utah, of course. He was in here yesterday askin' if anybody knew the feller.'

'That's mighty curious. Why should the man be doin' that?'

'He's a lawman, honeychile. Who knows? Maybe your brother's pard stole a chicken or somethin'.'

'That's loco talk. Clay Grady's one of the finest fellers I ever met.'

'Well, don't get riled, Lee. Let's talk about

somethin' else.'

Lee's scowl slowly began to fade. 'Like what for instance, Miss Kitty?'

'Why . . . like you and me makin' a night of it. Can we talk about that?'

He grinned broadly. 'Why not?' He hefted his glass. 'To a real big night, Miss Kitty.'

'Lookin' at you, sweetie.'

Saturday night in Apollo City was not proving as enjoyable for Luke Trafford as he had hoped. It had been pleasant enough during some preliminary beers taken at the Palace with Kentucky and several of the boys, and supper at the hotel with Virna and Tom had been just fine with no arguments to intrude on the good mood.

Following supper, he and Kentucky had gone along to the Three Aces to put in some serious drinking time at the long bar. And that was where Sheriff Clanton found them, immediately causing the fine evening to lose some of its glitter and shine.

Clanton was friendly and deferential but it was the questions he asked about Clay Grady that had first surprised, then irritated.

As did what the lawman put to him right now.

'It must seem mighty strange even to you that nobody else heard a thing about Grady's brush with the camp robbers at Rogue River, Luke?'

'Why should it? Grady didn't want to make a big fuss and we respected his wishes.'

'You didn't feel it should have been reported?'

'Clay asked us not to.'

'Do you mind telling me why?'

'If you must know, Sheriff, my pard got into some kind of a scrape back in Nevada. Nothing at all really, just something involving a cattleman's daughter. Women always pester Clay, he's that sort of man. Well, this girl's daddy was raising some hell and Clay just didn't want him bothering him after he'd been shot up and all. It's as simple as that.'

'You wouldn't happen to know this cattleman's name?'

Luke set his glass down on the bar.

'Look, I don't want to hear any more about Clay Grady. I don't know what's going on in your mind but you're barking up the wrong tree. Clay's as fine a man as I know.'

'I'm sure he is, Luke. But I'd still like to talk to him. Would it be all right with you if I came out to visit with him?'

'No, it damn well wouldn't! The man had a close scrape, Sheriff. He's still recovering and I'm not having him badgered by you or anybody else. When he's full recovered I'll have him ride in and see you, if you are still around. That's the best I can or will do.'

'Well . . . it sure isn't my job to annoy folks, Luke,' Clanton sighed, coming erect. 'I won't bother you any further. Much obliged for your time.'

'Doesn't that beat all, old-timer?' Luke growled as Clanton threaded his way off through the crowd. 'You don't suppose that lawman might somehow figure Clay was mixed up in that robbery, do you?'

'Who'd know?' Kentucky said thoughtfully. 'But I reckon when you stand back and look at things it is kind of strange nothin' more was heard of them camp robbers though. . . .'

'Don't you start up, old man. I came to town to ease up and relax, not listen to a whole lot of buffalo dust. C'mon, finish that drink and we'll go see if we can find the kid.'

'You're the boss, young Luke.'

Some time later after failing to locate Lee at any of the Main Street saloons the two decided he must be visiting friends. It never occurred to them to carry their search down to Crow Street where only the drunks and deadbeats congregated. And, because hunting around for his brother-in-law didn't come under the heading of things Luke Trafford most liked to do Saturday nights in town, they eventually quit the hunt and went looking for

122

action at the Palace.

They found it at a roulette wheel where Luke had his best run of luck in months. He also succeeded in getting old Kentucky slightly drunk while maintaining a clear head himself. And deciding that the night was finally beginning to take on the hoped-for pattern, he thrust everything else from his mind and concentrated exclusively on enjoying himself and, if possible, breaking the Palace's bank.

The ranch, the mine, the shipment, Tom and Virna, Lee and that nosy sheriff . . . they would all be still around come tomorrow.

He would worry about them then. Maybe.

Midnight at the Jimcrack Saloon was unlike midnight at any other drinking place in town. When you got drunk at the Jimcrack you were never thrown out. You simply slept at the table, or down on the boards if that was more convenient. And while you were busy doing nothing, percentage girls danced sleepily with lurching cowboys beneath smoking lights while the piano player beat out Camptown Races in the wrong key.

In truth the only person who looked stone cold sober to the eyes of Mallone and McCoy as they came through the batwings was the burly saloonkeeper behind the bar. He was the man making the money.

'What a pigsty!' McCoy disapproved, which was ironical. For McCoy was somebody who would not have appeared out of place in a real pigsty. With real pigs.

'So, we ain't here for the good of our health,' stated Mallone. He scanned the crowd and focused upon the young man and the sleeping girl at a table near the bar. 'That him?'

McCoy squinted through the tobacco haze. 'Uh huh. That's Lee Clarke.'

'Drunk?'

'Yup, looks like it.'

They sauntered over to the long bar and leaned against it. Lee didn't look up. Mallone ordered a whiskey and studied the boy with hooded eyes.

It had been a busy night for the bounty hunters during which they'd grown aware of Clanton's interest in the Maverick Ranch and a man named Clayton Grady. This in turn had triggered their own interest in the man. By now they knew the story of Grady's arrival on the spread and had heard the very significant piece of information that the man had arrived gunshot.

Indeed their interest had so sharpened they'd set out immediately to buddy up with several Maverick riders in order to learn more about the big spread and its guest, but with little luck. They were not the breed honest cowhands took to naturally at all. They did learn that Grady was still on the Maverick, but little besides. What they were mostly interested in was Lee Clarke, his present whereabouts and activities. From the description they furnished, McCoy recalled having sighted the man on Crow Street earlier that day.

Lee looked up blearily as the two arrived at his table toting drinks. He wasn't too sure what they looked like for the good reason he was too drunk.

'Have one with us, Lee,' Mallone asked amiably, taking a chair and pushing a glass across the table.

Lee struggled to focus. 'Do ... do I know you gents?'

'No, we're just drifters passin' through, down on our luck. Mallone and McCoy. Say, you look like somebody who might be down a little on his luck yourself, Lee.'

'No way. Never felt chirpier. Hey, Kitty, wake yourself up and meet Mallone and McCoy.'

Slumped gracefully in her chair, pretty Kitty snored. She wouldn't wake if the place caught fire.

So Mallone and McCoy felt free to go to work. They were friendly, bought more drinks, showed an interest in the Maverick Ranch. Lee was virtually incapable of intelligent conversation by this, but neither was he suspicious and surly towards them like most of the cowboys in the place. And when the name Clay Grady was finally raised by McCoy, he hoisted his glass and grinned.

'Fine feller that. Hey, c'mon and let's drink to old Clay.'

As they drank and the conversation continued, the pair ensured that Clay Grady remained the prime topic of conversation. Yet although amiable and likely flattered to have a couple of mature men so pleased to share his company, Lee was scarcely informative on the subject of Grady. Mostly he dwelt on Grady's exploits in the war as related by his uncle, Luke Trafford, along with what an excellent yarn-spinner the man was. But nothing they could really get their teeth into.

The bounty hunters were beginning to lose interest in him as an information source at just about the time Lee remembered his manners and insisted on treating them back. He went fishing in his pockets, then broke into a big grin.

'Hey, here I was thinkin' I was about busted, gents, but I've still got plenty!' He proceeded to unbutton his shirt front and with the air of a magician drawing a rabbit from a hat, produced a $100 bill. 'Next round's on me. Hell, every round's on me!'

Mallone went very still at sight of that big note. 'A man don't see many of them things around, Lee. You folks must be really flush out there on the spread these days.'

Lee leaned forward confidentially. 'Matter of fact, I've never had a hundred-dollar bill in my life, gents. Not before today, that is.'

'So, how come, kid?' Mallone probed. 'Get lucky at the tables?'

Lee shook his head slowly, grinning. 'Nope. But I can't tell you how I come by it. Promised I wouldn't.'

'Let me guess,' Mallone said in a low voice. 'This Grady gave it to you?'

Lee blinked in astonishment. 'How'd you figure that? Er, I mean . . . hell, I'm goin' to get another drink.' He knocked over his chair as he rose unsteadily. 'Hey, Jake, another three big ones!'

The bounty hunters traded a long stare as the boy weaved away.

'Pay dirt, you figure, Mallone?'

'Got to be, McCoy. That ten grand they stole from the Mercurio bank was all in $100 bills!'

'That's the truth, by hell! You know, suddenly I'm thinkin' you and me'd better stick close to this young feller, partner!'

'Close as a second skin – partner!'

NINE

GOLD ON THE MOVE

Virna tossed her head as she paced the front room in an ankle-length bathrobe, fretting about her brother. Everybody had returned to the spread from town expecting Lee to be with another party. She was infuriated that nobody seemed much concerned for the boy but herself. Before retiring Tom and Kentucky had made some whiskey-mellowed observations about a little fun and ruckusing being good for a growing boy, hinting diplomatically that she could not expect to keep him tied to her apron strings forever.

'He'll show, Virna,' Kentucky had reassured.

'Likely drunk as a skunk, but he'll show.'

As he did at last – one full hour later. She hurried outside in time to see two strangers helping her brother down from his horse.

'Lee!' she cried, and rushed down the steps.

'Mrs Trafford?' slurred the lean one. 'Now, don't go gettin' all upset, ma'am. The boy ain't done nothin' but get a little liquored. We just brung him home, is all.'

'And who might you be?' she demanded after seeing her brother was all right. Drunk, but unharmed.

'Jenner and Jackson, ma'am. Couple of hard-up punchers lookin' for a couple days' work to tide us over. Your brother hinted we might land a little odd-jobbin' hereabouts. Not that we're lookin' for any reward for bringin' him home safe, or nothin' like that, even if he was drunk as a skunk in town and kinda helpless. . . .'

'All right, all right, I'll discuss the work situation with my husband in the morning,' she said sharply. But then her manner softened as they half-carried her brother up the steps. 'I'm sorry to be so sharp. It's just that I was so concerned about my brother. It was really very kind for you to bring him all the way out here.'

'Our pleasure, ma'am,' insisted Mallone. 'He's a

right fine boy, we reckon. Just direct us to his room and we'll tote him in.'

'Thank you. But we must be quiet. We don't want to awaken the whole house. Everybody has had a strenuous night and there will be enough sore heads come morning as it is.'

'Quiet it'll be, ma'am,' grunted McCoy.

Virna realized just what a scruffy and rough-edged pair they were when they came in under the light, yet was so impressed with the gentle way they put her brother to bed that she refused to allow their appearance to bother her.

'The barn is over yonder,' she told them, ushering them back out onto the gallery. 'You will find plenty of clean straw and some old blankets. You should be quite comfortable for what's left of the night.'

Mallone jerked off his hat. 'Much obliged, Mrs Trafford. Er, you won't forget to ask your husband about them there jobs, will you? We'll tackle anythin'. Just a couple of days would see us right, ma'am.'

'I think I can promise you a couple of days' work,' she replied. 'It will be up to my husband to offer you any more than that.'

'I swear you are as fine a woman as your brother said, ma'am,' Mallone said humbly. 'And we are surely mighty beholden to you.'

'Mighty,' echoed McCoy. And he was being honest for once.

Luke rolled and lit his first cigarette of the new day. He regretted it immedately. His lungs seemed OK but his head was anything but.

And he asked himself – how come? What had tempted him to tie one on in town then end up catching no more than three hours' sleep on returning to the ranch?

For a moment he stood frowning and staring out over the acres from the front gallery. He knew why, he had to admit. There were tensions here at the headquarters and he'd set out to relieve them over a few shots and supposed he'd succeeded.

He turned as the front door banged open and Tom appeared looking a little puffy-eyed and pale but otherwise his usual bustling self.

'You plan to get a day's work in or stand around soaking up the good life?' Luke was asked.

'I beat you up by ten minutes.'

'The hell you—' Tom broke off sharply and touched fingers tenderly to temple. 'Man!' he groaned. 'I mean . . . why do we do it?'

Luke laughed. 'Who knows?' he replied. Then he sobered. 'Glad to see everybody got home OK.

Reckon we didn't set a great example on how relaxing country gents should behave in town, eh?'

'Speaking of relaxing . . . I'd like to be doing some right now but I've got to go see those fellers who brought the kid home last night. Want to come along?'

'Er . . . no.'

'What if I made it an order?' Tom half grinned.

'That'd be a huge mistake.'

Tom even managed a real smile as he strode off and Luke was grateful for time alone to pull himself together and do what he'd done every morning of his life since the signing at Appomattox Courthouse. Thank God that he and America had survived the greatest Civil War in history.

Then went looking for breakfast.

They were mucking out the stables next morning when Tom Trafford strode in. They saw that the rancher was not impressed with their appearance and figured they were likely lucky that he was suffering from a hangover and therefore chose the quick way of dealing with them to get it over with.

'My wife tells me we're in your debt,' he said grumpily.

'Not at all, Mr Trafford,' Mallone insisted, whipping off his hat. 'We only done what we would have done for anybody. But it was mighty good of your wife to give us a couple of days' work ... mighty good.'

'Hmm. Well, all right, I guess it's the least we can do. You eaten yet?'

'Not yet – boss.'

'There's grub at the cookhouse,' Trafford grunted, and left.

The two were sauntering across to the cookshack a short time later when they sighted two tall men emerge from the ranch house. One was Luke Trafford, his companion a handsome and dark-headed man puffing on a cigar.

Instantly Mallone turned his face away and kept it averted until they were safely inside the cookshack. He then hurried to the window to peer out at the house. A puzzled McCoy ranged up alongside.

'What is it, Mallone? You know this feller?'

Mallone couldn't conceal his excitement.

'One'll get you ten that this is our Clay Grady. But that ain't his only name. He was Shane Wallace up in Wyomin' Territory a year back when he robbed a bank and killed a teller. Another dollar will get you ten that he's our fourth man, partner.'

'Well I be damned!'

'So will he, McCoy, so will he. But not yet. Afore we spring this trap we got to find out what shifty game this varmint's playing here. And we got to find out where he's stashed the stolen dinero.'

'Does this owl hoot know you, Mallone?'

'That he does. So you can bet I'll be makin' double certain he don't spot me. We won't poke our snouts out of that stable by daylight.'

'Dangerous one, huh?'

'They don't come more dangerous, McCoy. This pilgrim kills quicker than a rattler.'

McCoy swallowed as he thought back to their grisly find in Lizard Desert. He felt a twinge of simple envy as he studied Mallone's smiling face. He wasn't worried one lick, likely due to the fact there was a lot of pure rattlesnake in his makeup also.

McCoy turned back to the room and realized the cook and several ranch hands were staring at them curiously. He gave Mallone a warning nudge and they slouched across to the counter wearing big grins.

'Howdy, gents,' Mallone said amiably. 'The boss-man put us to swampin' the stables for a couple of days. What's best on your meal ticket today, cookie?'

'Stew,' replied Tad Gruber, and turned away to fill a couple of plates.

Zac Stannard stared hard as the two turned away from the counter. 'Hey, ain't you the fellers what was hangin' about the Palace yesterday askin' a mess of questions about the Maverick?'

'Correct, pard,' Mallone answered easily. 'Didn't let on then, but we were fishin' to find out if there might be a job or two goin' out here.' He tapped his chest. 'I'm Jackson. This here is Jenner.'

There was an uncertain moment. The bounty hunters had been careful not to reveal their real names in Apollo City. But there was some risk that Ben Clanton might have mentioned who they really were.

They only began to breathe easier when the cowboys just nodded their heads indifferently and returned to their meal. The bounty hunters slipped into a corner table and looked about warily.

'Seems we sure better stay real close to them there stables, Mallone.'

'Right close, McCoy. Any snoopin' that's to be done today, you can do it. I'll only come out at night. Like a weasel.'

'What if Grady lucks onto you?'

'He dies. Now, eat up, man, eat up.'

The escort from Phoenix's Cattlemen's Bank arrived at Maverick headquarters late the following afternoon, two men mounted and two riding on the bank's armor-plated bullion wagon drawn by four sturdy bay horses.

Rory Kilrain, ex-soldier and ex-Pinkerton man, was in charge, a burly and competent professional who specialized in this kind of high-security work for the Cattlemen's Bank.

His crew as always were carefully hand-picked. Sickles was senior security supervisor from the bank while Priest and Walters were both full-time shotgun guards with the Cattlemen's transport interests.

It was Kilrain's sixth visit to Maverick and the Traffords welcomed him like an old friend. His men were put up at the bunkhouse overnight but Kilrain himself was given a room in the east wing of the house next door to Grady's.

After refreshments were taken at the house, Tom and Luke took Kilrain down to the gold room where they inspected the bullion and made final arrangements for next day. After that there was supper followed by brandy and cigars. It was some time later when Clay Grady drew Luke aside to tell him he'd reached a decision.

It was time he moved on.

He explained that listening to Kilrain talk about Phoenix had seen him come down with a hankering for new sights and fresh faces. He liked the sound of Phoenix and if it was all right with Luke he'd travel south to Phoenix with the escort. And who could tell? Maybe if he made himself useful on the escort Kilrain might use his good offices to secure him employment down south?

Though taken by surprise by the sudden decision, Luke could come up with no genuine objections. And thinking about that scene he'd witnessed between Clay and Virna, Luke knew it was time Clay moved on.

'Place won't see the same without you, Clay,' he said after a silence. 'You've done us all a power of good just being here.'

'I sure hope that's the truth, Luke. But we must be honest with one another, old pard. You know my style of old. Leave me too long in any one place and I'm just naturally going to raise the dust and land in trouble one way or the other. I'm a born freewheeler and it's high time I was moving on. So, let's go see Tom, huh?'

Tom took some convincing about the new arrangements for he was a man who liked everything cut and dried when he made plans, particularly where shipments were concerned. But after Luke convinced him that a man of Clay Grady's capabilities could only prove a big asset to the escort, he eventually gave in and it became official: Grady would travel south with the gold wagon next day.

This occasion called for more drinks. Tom Trafford expected Virna to be disappointed when she came in and heard the news, yet she wasn't. If anything, she appeared relieved and, watching her, Grady realized this was one woman who'd proven impervious to the Grady charm.

Not that any of this was of any consequence now.

Grady had what he wanted and had a busy night ahead of him after the party broke up. He had been reluctant to quit Maverick alone with his cache because of the possible risk of meeting the lawmen who might still be hunting for him. Yet no lawman would have any cause to look twice at an upstanding citizen traveling south with a gold escort.

Phoenix lay eight miles south. Once safely there he would make the remainder of the way to Old Mexico alone.

That night saw the wartime pards get together for a farewell drink. The mood was sober, the air filled with recollections of a past where men were slaughtered in their hundreds and thousands and it was miracle when two pards survived the madness together.

Yet while they talked and reminisced out on the long gallery Luke felt prey to an unexpected feeling of almost relief that Grady was going.

How come?

He examined his emotions and came up with something both extraordinary and totally unwelcome. For he was realizing at last that their time together here had been very different from that which they'd shared upon the bloodiest battlefield in human history.

Analyzing this further he realized they'd either both changed greatly in that relatively brief time of peace or had been essentially different from the outset without being aware of it.

He studied Grady objectively and saw a man who seemed like a stranger, immensely harder and maybe far more dangerous than he'd ever realized.

Just like a stranger. . . .

He shook his head at the thought and Grady paused in what he was saying to stare at him questioningly.

'You OK, Luke?'

'Huh?'

'You just looked kind of . . . well, different, I guess. Like you'd just had a shock, maybe.'

Luke studied the man and thought what a fool he'd be to allow uncertainty and doubt to intrude on a friendship of such long standing.

He stuck out his right hand.

Clayton Grady grabbed it in silence and the

feeling between them was just like before the battle again, solid, strong and sure.

They parted at that point with Grady revealing he intended taking a short night ride before turning in: 'Sort of to say goodbye properly to the place that saved my life . . . not just rush it in the morning. '*Compré*, Luke?'

'Sure, Clay. Ride safe.'

The headquarters had fallen quiet twenty minutes later when Grady rode out. He turned behind the hay barn under the moon then struck west across moonwashed rangeland for several miles before veering sharply southeast.

It was midnight when he reached Coyote Gulch.

He rode directly to a gnarled patch of mesquite standing behind a cluster of stones on the south side of a narrow little gulch.

He reined in and swung down.

The first time he'd seen this tree it had not been still as it was now but rather twisting and buckling in his distorted vision.

He remembered the enormous effort it had cost to rip his saddle apart and extract the wads of banknotes which he'd stuffed into the lining that night in the Sawbuck Hills before setting his henchmen's horses loose and taking flight.

After caching the money in a crevice behind the mesquite that night he had collapsed, woken several hours later, then staggered away, still toting his saddle as he'd done throughout his journey from Lizard Desert. There was no reason to carry the saddle now but he was still in a delirium he'd fought against with all his strength before passing out the final time somewhere upon the east graze of the Maverick Ranch, where the ranch hands had come upon him at dawn.

Naturally he had been back to check out the cache to find it safe and secure, as he did again now.

It took time to once more rip out the stuffing of his saddle and pack it again, tight and neat, with wads of large-denomination banknotes. If an idea worked once it had to be good for a second time.

The old feeling of drunken excitement returned in full as he rode back to the spread. The feeling that he was a giant walking in a world of pygmies. Times like this it was like being immortal and knowing there was no way he could lose.

When he reached headquarters he rode directly into the stables, swung down and went inside to put up the horse. The night lamp burned low.

Horses nodded drowsily from the stalls.

Stripping off the saddle he toted it across to the light and carefully inspected his hasty handiwork with needle and twine. Seeing a section where the stitching had already worked a little loose during the ride in, he took the bag needle from his shirt pocket and lowered himself onto a stool to make repairs.

The night wind blew and old boards creaked. His expression was intent as he worked and he heard nothing until the gun muzzle touched between his shoulder blades and the voice said quietly:

'Blink and you're dead, Grady. Or should that be Wallace?'

Grady's entire body locked. It felt as if his blood had turned to icy red crystals and he was no longer feeling like any kind of giant. His eyes rolled sideways and he glimpsed a burly, bearded figure moving to come around before him with a big Navy Colt in his fist and a crooked smile.

Grady blinked.

He didn't understand.

For this was one of the two bums who'd brought the Trafford kid back home drunk from Apollo City. Then the second man appeared from the shadows, and he nodded. It was them all right. Rough as dirt and likely dangerous as the cholera.

He stared into the hawk face of Mallone and felt the force of the man's personality.

'Been a time since Wyomin',' Mallone smirked.

'McCoy, get his Colt, then take a gander at this here saddle he seems to have took such a shine to.'

McCoy obediently plucked the Colt from the holster then handed Grady a backhander that belted him clear off the stool. 'You've given us a hard time of it, Grady,' he smirked, holstering the Colt and lifting the fat saddle. 'We'd nigh give you up for lost.'

Grady knew he was a dead man as he lay trussed and gagged watching the two rip his saddle apart to reveal the money. They'd crossed trails once before and knew what he was. They taunted him by telling him they'd figured all along that he'd had the money stashed, that it was just a matter of time before he'd go recover it.

'Let's make a deal, Mallone.'

'No deals. Anyway, you got nothin' to deal with, loser.'

Staring death in the face, Grady felt his brain kick into top gear. He began to talk and talked fast. The ten grand was theirs, he declared. It was just chicken feed – small change. Nothing compared to the thirty thousand in gold the Traffords were shipping to Phoenix tomorrow. He had planned to grab the lot but under the circumstances now was willing to make it a three-way cut. Ten thousand apiece. And he could show them how he could achieve it simply by capitalizing on his friendship with Luke Trafford.

The bounty hunters were suspicious at first. Yet they listened. Who wouldn't for thirty grand?

'Keep talkin, Grady,' McCoy growled, and Clayton Grady, war hero, killer and thief talked like never before.

He'd been planning to take the big gold shipment from the day he'd first learned of it. Had studied the proposed route, planned to make full use of his friendship with Luke Trafford to pull it off . . . just exactly how he hadn't been sure. But three of them – plus some hand-picked backing? Money for old rope!

They still didn't trust him. Yet the longer he talked the less skeptical they became. The money was huge, the risks enormous, yet Clayton Grady had the look and the talk and the ice-cold confidence of a man who just might be able to take on the biggest heist they'd ever dreamed of.

So they let him talk. He would be riding with the gold escort tomorrow as the Traffords' trusted friend, he revealed. Luke Trafford was the danger man so he would take him out of the equation at a designated time and place where his new partners and their bunch would be waiting to move in – shooting.

Sure, there would be plenty of risk. Only a fool would doubt that. But with Luke dead and the three of them against the escort . . . if that wasn't a chance worth grabbing he'd never heard of one.

The pair at last holstered their guns away and settled down to go over the plan again and again . . . while their new partner smiled with relief inside. . . .

Once again, the yawning grave that had been waiting for Clayton Grady all his violent life had been avoided. He had seldom felt more excitingly alive than now, seated there in the lamplight in the barn calmly plotting the murder of eight men including the one man living who believed him to be a true friend.

The gold escort was ready to roll and daylight was breaking over Maverick Ranch.

Big Tom rested a hand on Lee's shoulder. 'I'm leaving you in charge, boy. You and Kentucky. And you know, I reckon I couldn't leave the Maverick in better hands.'

Watching Lee's face flush with pride, Grady turned to find Kentucky staring fixedly at him. The old-timer looked sober as he bade the escort party farewell.

'You take care now, young Luke.'

'You too.'

'Look, I gotta say this, boy, though it don't pleasure me none. But I've never cottoned to your pard and it gives me an uneasy feelin' to see him ridin' out with you today—'

Luke didn't listen any further. Yet because of the old timer's words, felt a twinge almost of unease as they rode out and struck south. Sometimes, he thought to himself, crazy old men should keep their thoughts to themselves. Not trust Clay? Loco!

The heat blasted down.

Luke Trafford struck a lucifer into life and applied the flame to the tip of the cigarette jutting from his teeth. He drew deep, grimaced. Tobacco was supposed to relax this odd tension he'd been experiencing ever since the party had entered Warcloud Valley but plainly was having no effect. Just like the last cigarette he'd tossed away only a minute before.

What was it working on his nerves anyway? He'd not felt like this since the war. Damnit . . . it felt almost like being *back* in the war at places like Peat's Bridge, Amtucket Sound, Silverado Ridge. . . .

He hipped around in the saddle. Three men rode a short distance behind, flanking the gold wagon. Two were grimacing in the heat and dust but the third, Grady, was smiling as he threw him a lazy salute.

For a moment a chill came over him as understanding struck home. Grady! That was what felt wrong. But what in the Sam Hill did he mean by *that*?

TEN

NO HERO
LIES HERE

The iron-rimmed wheels of the gold wagon clattered against stone as it rumbled across the dry wash and began to climb the steep slope beyond. Leveling out again, the trail continued in a series of gentle curves with banks rising high on either side before flattening toward the tight turn some half-mile ahead.

'Devil's Hairpin soon,' the burly driver grunted to the man seated beside him on the spring seat. 'We're makin' good time.'

Grady took out a cigar and lighted it. He rode relaxed in the saddle with only his eyes restlessly scanning the sweltering landscape on either side of the rough trail.

He was riding to the left of the wagon with Luke Trafford on the opposite side. Tom and Kilrain were up front while two horsemen brought up the rear.

Clayton Grady's eyes cut past the squat, armor-plated bullion box which was strongly bolted to the wagon floor, and glimpsed Luke Trafford building a cigarette one-handed.

Sometimes he marveled that a man as trusting and unquestioning as Trafford had survived the war. This hardcase didn't trust a living soul. Yet straight-shooting Luke had never suspected this characteristic in him, so he believed. Luke was a man who liked to believe the best of everyone. They'd become friends in the war largely on account Trafford had saved Grady's life on several occasions. But that meant little or nothing to Grady in the long term. Several years post-war, he'd made contact with Trafford without knowing he had a rich family in back of him. But from the day he'd arrived at Maverick, Grady had been plotting to exploit the Trafford clan, knew he'd found the way, the time and the place the day he'd first learned about the shipment to the south.

He'd kill his own mother for a tenth of what was riding on this slow wagon.

The bend was just a few hundred yards ahead by now. Grady cleared his mind of all distracting thoughts and emotions and concentrated totally on what the next minutes would bring once they rounded Devil's Hairpin.

Beyond the bend waited the scum and saloon sweepings he'd recruited, hardcases for the big heist. He'd smelled the owlhoot stink on Mallone and McCoy as strong as rat poison from the very beginning, and recruiting the pair had been almost too easy. He'd promised them a half-cut and it had almost made him laugh in their faces the greedy and eager way they'd trusted him. Their 'cut' would be delivered by his .45.

The walls of the Hairpin loomed. Grady reached inside his jacket and the .45 filled his hand with a thrill that never lessened for him. Another thirty yards and they were rounding the curve when without warning the roar of rifle shots shattered the day and masked riders erupted from nowhere, brandishing rifles and shouting at the wagon driver to halt – all in the space of seconds.

Instinctively, automatically, an outrider flanking the wagon swung up his rifle only to be driven backwards under a scything hail of outlaw lead that instantly transformed Devil's Hairpin into a scene of slaughterhouse chaos.

Through those first chaotic moments as weapons raged and thundered and a mortally hit man screamed like a woman, Luke Trafford could smell death in the very air stronger and more sickeningly than at any time since it had been a daily part of his life on the grisly battlefields of Shiloh, Mechanicsville and murderous Gettysburg.

And in that searing instinct, the veteran who'd struck back against the grey hordes in those hells-on-earth in the Great War was already fighting back, blasting murderously at the smoke-shrouded shadows of men with weapons, ducking and twisting violently in his saddle yet somehow managing to control his mount with the pressure from his knees while he fired, fired then fired again before the animal crashed down from underneath him to strike with brutal impact and he went spinning into blackness.

Was he still unconscious?

That was Luke's first thought as he came up on one knee in deep gloom, a darkness that he slowly realized was caused by the thick dust boiling around him where he lay sprawled and blinking up at the sturdy under-frame of the gold wagon!

Violently, angrily, he kicked his way between what looked like giant wheels, then coughing and choking but all the time powering forward now, he came out from under and shot a lunging stranger squarely in the face at close range – a stranger wearing a robber's black mask.

Madness ruled around him as he barely avoided being trampled by a fear-maddened horse, the blast of gunfire at close quarters deafening with ghostly figures surging through the roiling dust on all sides, some shooting, some howling, all like himself deafened by the insane clash of arms . . . the Great War again, three years on!

He jumped a corpse, powered towards an open space, tripped and crashed heavily to ground. Again. Rising on one knee he found himself blinking into the face of a dead driver at close quarters.

This really was the war all over again!

For just a frightening moment this thought consumed him. But next instant he was cold and calm and springing to his feet. Not a moment too soon. A horse and rider came surging out of the swirling madness and the blast of a revolver was so close it all but deafened him. He reeled backwards and swung up his .45 as a gust of wind momentarily cleared the air and he was staring up at a rearing horse, its rider clutching a smoking gun that was sweeping downwards at him!

He had one split-second out of eternity to whip up the .45 and trigger once, twice, three times, each shot following the other so swiftly that the sound was a continuous rolling roar.

None of the three bullets missed Clayton Grady.

For Luke Trafford there was one searing moment of total disbelief, incomprehension and denial as, with hot crimson spilling from the cruel holes in chest and head, the big body plummeted to bare ground almost at his feet to roll downslope slowly, bleeding all the way.

The figure that had emerged from beneath the bullet-riddled gold wagon was dust-coated, hollow-eyed, but still shooting.

He cut down a total stranger with his first bullet then helped a wounded Maverick hand finish off a man in a red shirt wearing a mask.

Luke staggered as he swung away in search of another target, only to realize slowly that the deafening roar of weaponry had ceased, giving way now abruptly to different sounds ... somebody moaning in mortal agony ... an injured animal struggling to rise ... a single shot close by ... the clatter of a runaway horse ... and then the final shot.

He didn't recognize it as such for the moments it

took for the dust and gunsmoke to begin to clear. He realized that the only haggard, hollow-eyed men to be seen moving amongst the wounded and dead now were Maverick hands, amongst them, staring at him hollow-eyed and speechless from some thirty feet away, his brother Tom and, invincible as ever, the lean shape of Old Kentucky. 'Thought you might need a hand,' the old-timer grunted.

Standing gaping at a chaotic scene that might have been a Civil War battlefield Luke finally comprehended that the madness was over. The overturned wagon was half-wrecked but a sturdy figure clutching a rifle loomed wide-legged against the clearing sky with a shotgun in his hands, still standing guard.

He might have smiled but for the fact that in that moment he felt like somebody who would never smile again, as he went looking for Clayton Grady.

The shadows were closing in.

Propped up against a bullet-scarred boulder at trailside and dragging on his last cigarette as he stared away from the battle scene at the serene and distant hills, Clayton Grady coughed blood and almost smiled.

'Don't take it so serious, Luke,' he said quietly. 'I played the game my way and the dice rolled against me. Luck of the draw. How many times did we see that in the war?'

'But why? We were pards in the war – my family treated you like a king when you showed up—'

'If you stop jawing, I'll tell you. And believe me I don't have much time left.'

'I'm listening,' Luke muttered, astonished to realize how much this was hurting. This man dabbing at the trickle of blood coming from his mouth had betrayed their friendship, caused good men to die. And yet he already knew he was going to miss him. So, how come?

'I was straight in the war on account the excitement never ended there. After the war was different. I had to have excitement and . . . and the best way to find it was with a gun.' A shrug. 'Believe it or not, I only came upon you by chance, three years on. Also likely hard to believe is that I looked you up just to see you again. I didn't realize your family was so rich until later . . . but straightaway I was planning how to get my hands on some of the big dinero. . . .'

'But,' Luke protested, 'that wasn't—'

The sentence was never finished. With a slight cough and a half-grin, Clay Grady dropped his chin to his chest and was gone.

Luke couldn't believe it . . . none of it. There was

no knowing how long he sat there frozen by shock, disbelief and a contradictory feeling of great loss.

He didn't glance up until a hand fell on his shoulder. Kentucky nodded. 'Best this way, Luke. C'mon, we got lots to do.'

'But Clay. . . .' he protested, getting up.

'Is at peace now,' the veteran said quietly. 'The only way men of his kind can find it, I guess.'

And that was Clayton Grady's valedictory.

Sheriff Ben Clanton was a thorough man and that same quality manifested itself in the days following the murderous gun battle at Devil's Hairpin.

McCoy, having survived a belly wound, proved of great assistance to the lawman in putting all the pieces together concerning how Grady had organized the robbery, recruited the gang, bending over backwards in his eagerness to tell all in the hope of merely drawing prison time instead of the hang-rope he deserved for the part he'd played in the bullion robbery.

McCoy's testimony in conjunction with Sheriff Clanton's ride out to Lizard Desert to locate the remains of the dead outlaws, and supported further by what the lawman learned from the Traffords, enabled him to make a full and accurate report on the Mercurio robbery before marking the case closed.

Being the thorough man he was, Clanton wired all details of the affair through to headquarters in Mercurio with the request that certain matters relating to it should be referred onwards to the marshals' headquarters in Salt Lake City.

The day the replies reached him in Apollo City was the day he rode out, in thoughtful mood, to visit Maverick Ranch.

He found things virtually back to normal. These were strong people who had been through hell and Clanton wasn't surprised to their quick recovery. Part of his reason for visiting the spread before heading on home to headquarters, was to inform Luke Trafford what he had learned about his former friend, which he did over drinks with the family and old Kentucky in the big front room of the ranch house.

Salt Lake City had supplied Clanton with information that Clayton Grady had gone directly from the army at war's end to ride with the Missouri Raiders at the start of an outlaw career that had seen him ply his trade across the West over several years which included a three-year stretch in Yuma Prison.

His theory was that, like so many other veterans, Grady had been exposed to such excitement and bloodshed during the war years he'd found the prospect of peace and order untenable, a notion Luke already believed to be true.

It was only a short time after this that Tom Trafford made the decision to shut down the mine and take his wife east to New York on a second honeymoon, leaving his brother in charge.

That evening as a soft dusk came down over the spread Luke Trafford stood a little apart from the revelers come for the send-off and saw everything as it could and should be – the finest cattle spread in the county, no outlaws, no feuding, and, maybe best of all, no goddamn mining!

It wasn't until he heard a sound behind that he turned to see Virna looking lovelier than ever and smiling at Tom in a way he'd never seen before, that he realized he'd overlooked the single most important aspect of all. The love between husband and wife.

He'd rearranged all his thinking and his priorities in just those bare seconds in realizing what was missing from his own life – a wife like Virna to call his own. And watching from the shadows unseen, Old Kentucky nodded and smiled. For a time it had seemed that all the misunderstanding, stubbornness and bloodshed visited upon this place he loved so deeply might have continued until the end of his days.

The way things were shaping now, however, he figured he might well feel free to go to his rest any time he wanted. Not happy maybe, but free.

Only thing, he now felt so fine he knew he never would want to leave. A man would have to be loco to quit this life . . . now.

Library Link Issues (For Staff Use Only)

1	2	3	4	5	6	7	8	9
		326A			669A			